DATE DUE			
12-3-94			

Jackson
County
Library
System

HEADQUARTERS:

413 W. Main

Medford, Oregon   97501

Theodore Roosevelt Takes Charge

The many sides of Theodore Roosevelt.

Theodore Roosevelt Takes Charge

Nancy Whitelaw

Albert Whitman & Company • Morton Grove, Illinois

Special thanks to Wallace Finley Dailey, Curator, Theodore Roosevelt Collection, Harvard College Library; Kathleen Young, Museum Aid, Sagamore Hill National Historic Site; and Doris Ursitti, Assistant Curator, The Theodore Roosevelt Inaugural National Historic Site, for their help in providing photographs.

Library of Congress Cataloging-in-Publication Data

Whitelaw, Nancy.
   Theodore Roosevelt takes charge / Nancy Whitelaw.
   p. cm.
   Summary: Describes the life of the twenty-sixth president of the United States, from his sickly youth through his varied career as rancher, author, and politician.
   ISBN: 0-8075-7849-5
   1. Roosevelt, Theodore, 1858-1919—Juvenile literature. 2. Presidents—United States—Biography—Juvenile literature. [1. Roosevelt, Theodore, 1858-1919. 2. Presidents.] I. Title.
E757.W58   1992
973.91′1′092—dc20
[B]
[92]   90-29181
                                       CIP
                                       AC

For Dave, my favorite history teacher

Contents

Chapter 1
The Fateful Camping Trip

The first half of Friday the thirteenth in September 1901 is a good luck day for Theodore Roosevelt, vice-president of the United States.

Roosevelt and his friends congratulate each other. After a long climb, they have reached the top of the highest peak in the Adirondack Mountains of New York State.

The second half of that Friday is a like a bad dream. The campers are munching on sandwiches around two o'clock when a woodsman comes puffing up the trail, waving a yellow telegram.

Guessing the message before he receives the telegram, the vice-president is stunned. Three days before, he had left President William McKinley's bedside, certain that the president would soon recover from the bullet wound of a would-be assassin. In fact, advisers had urged him to leave the wounded president to show the American people that their leader was out of danger.

The message comes from Elihu Root, secretary of war, who wires from Buffalo, New York: "The President appears to be dying and members of the Cabinet in Buffalo think you should lose no time in coming."

Roosevelt during his vice-presidency.

The president—our William McKinley—"Appears to be dying"—the doctors weren't sure! "Lose no time in coming"—how long ago was that written?

Hurry! Down the steep and narrow trail. Through the slippery mud. Over the sharp rocks.

Four hours later, Roosevelt and the messenger reach the foot of the mountain. But they are still four hundred miles from Buffalo where President McKinley is...what? Recovering? Dying? Dead?

A courier is sent to the nearest telephone, six miles away, to arrange for a buckboard wagon to take the vice-president to North Creek where he can catch a train to Buffalo.

At eleven o'clock that night, the rickety buckboard arrives. The night sky is dark and starless as Roosevelt climbs onto the wagon.

That buckboard ride is a Friday the thirteenth nightmare. The wagon bounces and jounces over bumps and ruts, and it slips and slides through muddy puddles. No guard rails outline the sharp curves of the narrow dirt road. No lights reveal the slender shoulder between the wagon and the steep drop-off.

The vice-president urges Mike, the driver, to go faster, whether he can see or not. They must reach North Creek by daylight!

As the buckboard careens around another sharp corner, dirt and pebbles and mud splatter against it. Roosevelt holds on by grabbing the edge of the seat with one hand and the seat arm with the other. The two men bounce up and then back down again onto the hard wooden bench. Mike cracks the whip over the rain-soaked backs of the horses as they speed into the night.

Six hours later, in the faint light of the rising sun, the two men see steam rising from the waiting locomotive as they pull into North Creek.

The engineer recognizes Roosevelt. Probably he has seen some of the cartoons that exaggerate Roosevelt's two-hundred-pound muscular body, his rimless glasses, and his large, even white teeth under a bushy mustache.

The engineer removes his hat as he approaches the wagon.

William Loeb, one of Roosevelt's secretaries, is waiting on the train. He says, "The president died at two-fifteen this morning."

Roosevelt climbs aboard the two-car train. In about seven hours he will be in Buffalo. And shortly after that, on this fourteenth day of September 1901, Theodore Roosevelt will become the twenty-sixth president of the United States.

─────────────────────────────────

An artist's drawing shows Roosevelt taking the oath of office in Buffalo on September 14, 1901.

Chapter 2
Bugs, Birds, and Four-Legged Animals

Theodore Roosevelt was born on October 27, 1858.

"He looks like a turtle," Mittie Roosevelt said as she inspected her newborn son, Theodore Roosevelt, Jr.

Some months later, this "turtle" was getting into mischief at a speed that wore out his mother and father, his older sister Anna (called "Bamie"), and the four servants who lived with them in their New York City home.

His mother was a Southerner. The former Martha Bulloch was a black-haired beauty and a popular hostess in New York society circles. Mittie, as she was called, often told the children happy stories of her early life on a plantation in Roswell, Georgia, surrounded by family and slaves. Mittie suffered from poor health most of her life, and the children learned to be very gentle with her, just as their father was.

The new baby's father nicknamed his son "Teedie." Theodore Roosevelt, Sr. was a Northerner, a wealthy glass merchant, a generous man. He founded the New York Orthopedic Hospital, perhaps partly in an attempt to help Bamie, who was born with a spinal problem. He also founded the Children's Aid Society to place city orphans in country

Teedie, aged four years.

Theodore Roosevelt, Sr.

homes. Years later, Governor Brady of the Alaska Territory greeted Theodore Roosevelt, Jr. (then governor of New York), saying, "Your father picked me up from the streets in New York, a waif and an orphan . . . and now I am a fellow governor."

Teedie's father volunteered many hours at the Newsboys' Lodging House where homeless youngsters, mostly newsboys, could sleep in a clean bed in a warm room for five cents a night. He raised money to support this home.

Theodore Roosevelt, Sr., taught his children by example that each person has a duty to mankind. Free from financial worries because of his successful business, he spent many hours working on projects to help the needy and to raise money for hospitals and museums. He said, "I feel that as much as I enjoy loafing, there is something higher for which to live."

Martha Bulloch Roosevelt.

In the business world, Theodore Roosevelt, Sr., was known for his determination. When he wanted something, he usually got it.

The Civil War might have torn apart a weaker marriage. Mittie's family kept slaves; Theodore disapproved of slavery. Mittie supported the Confederacy; Theodore paid for a substitute (a common practice) to fight for him on the Union side. He explained that he feared he might find himself in battle against Mittie's relatives. This family controversy deepened after Mittie's mother and sister Annie moved in with Theodore and Mittie.

But Theodore found a way to help the Union cause when he heard that many families of soldiers became destitute when their wage-earners went away to war. He met with congressmen, and even with President Abraham Lincoln, to persuade them to support a bill encouraging soldiers to send part of their pay home. After this bill passed, he traveled

Lincoln's funeral procession in New York City, April 1865.
It is thought that Teedie and Elliott are the children looking
out the second-story window of the house with shutters.

on horseback from camp to camp, impressing upon soldiers the importance of supporting their families at home.

After the war, he worked with the Soldiers' Employment Bureau where he helped injured veterans to find work.

Teedie was aware of this North vs. South family conflict although his parents tried to keep their differences from their children. Once Teedie was angry with his mother, and he decided to get back at her when he said prayers with her that night. He prayed for victory of the Union forces, adding, "And I hope God will grind the Southern forces to powder."

The Civil War was, indeed, threatening to grind the whole country to powder. First the South, then the North appeared to be winning. In fact, the whole country was losing as Americans fought and killed each other and destroyed buildings and land.

When he was just seven, Teedie watched the funeral procession for assassinated president Abraham Lincoln as it passed solemnly through the streets of New York. The president had been shot just five days after the war had ended.

Teedie was a sickly child. He caught cold easily, and he spent a lot of time in bed, shaking and sweating with high temperatures and coughing until his throat and chest were sore. When he vomited and had diarrhea, he said, "I have toothache in my stomach."

His most serious illness was asthma. Whether he was running a race or sitting still with a book, Teedie never knew when he would suddenly find himself struggling for breath. Perhaps most terrifying, he would wake up in the middle of the night nearly suffocating, and without enough breath to call to his parents. Years later, he remembered the agony, and he wrote: "One of my memories is of my father walking up and down the room with me in his arms at night when I was a very small person, and of sitting up in bed gasping."

"He won't live another year," predicted his Aunt Annie, shaking her head over Teedie's pale complexion and scrawny body.

When an asthma attack left him weak, Teedie sat in a small red velvet chair in the huge, dark library behind the parlor. He studied the illustrations—giraffes, zebras, antelopes, and elephants—in a favorite book. He loved to look at drawings of insects, too, especially the ones of a tsetse fly.

After a while, he would become impatient with not being able to read the words. Off he would go, dragging the book from room to room, looking for an adult to read to him. For a few years, his Aunt Annie read to him often. But by the time Teedie was four years old, his aunt was also helping care for his younger brother, Elliott ("Ellie"), and his baby sister, Corinne ("Conie").

Soon Teedie could not satisfy his curiosity with pictures. He needed to explore for himself. He began to bring the world of nature home to his bedroom. First it was an exceptionally pretty rock, a colorful feather, and a few leaves. Then he added a snakeskin, some bits of fur, and a bird wing. Teedie arranged his collection neatly on shelves and then added a sign, "The Roosevelt Museum of Natural History."

Perhaps he was inspired by his father, whom he admired. Theodore, Sr., helped to establish both the American Museum of Natural History and the Metropolitan Museum of Art. The senior Roosevelt generously gave both time and money for these causes. His son said of him, "No one whom I have ever met approached his combination of enjoyment of life and performance of duty."

Every summer the Roosevelt family vacationed in the country. There Teedie added to his museum collection. He learned to move quickly and quietly to catch turtles, snakes, and lizards. He spent hours splashing around in search of minnows, frogs, and salamanders. He listened intently to the songs of thrushes, sparrows, and other birds, and soon he could identify many birds by their calls.

The day he saw a dead seal was the day he decided to become a zoologist. The animal lay stretched out on a plank in the Broadway marketplace not far from Teedie's home. A storekeeper was displaying the seal to attract the attention of customers. Seven-year-old Teedie asked the storekeeper if he could study it. The man replied that he could—if he could stand the smell.

Teedie paid no attention to the smell. He immediately took out a folding pocket ruler and tried to wrap it around the sides and belly of the seal. In his autobiography, he describes this project: "I carefully made a record of utterly useless measurements, and at once began to write a natural history." Too soon for Teedie, the carcass smelled so bad that the storekeeper threw it out. Just in time, Teedie asked if he could have the skull. He displayed it proudly in his museum.

When he was nine, Teedie filled forty pages of a notebook with descriptions of animals and insects. He wrote about three different kinds of ants. One was the shiny ant, "pure black except the officer who is striped with yellow. It is pretty common. It eats flies, mosquitos, etc. They sometimes have fights with spiders." He also wrote about the darning needle which "has brown transparent wings through which you can read writing. Its color is bluish green. There is a foolish superstition about its sewing up peoples' cheeks which I scarcely need add is not true." He titled his book "Natural History on Insects."

The more Teedie learned, the more curious he became. Soon his museum overflowed into the rest of the house. His mother found a litter of field mice in the icebox. The cook refused to follow Teedie's directions to boil a woodchuck, fur and all, for twenty-four hours. Once when Teedie lifted his hat in respect to a family friend, a frog leaped off the top of his head.

In 1869, when Teedie was ten, Theodore, Sr., and Mittie planned a family trip to Europe to extend the education the children received from home tutors. Like many wealthy families of that time, the Roosevelts decided to stay abroad for about a year. In May, they left on a paddle-steamer for Liverpool, England. Teedie cried all way to the pier; he did not want to be away from home for so long.

Teedie was seasick during most of the ten-day trip across the Atlantic Ocean. His only pleasure during that time was sighting porpoises, dolphins, gulls, and a shark. Arriving on land didn't help much because then he became homesick.

Worse, he suffered from asthma attacks. Every few days, the attacks left him ill, weak, and depressed. His anxious parents tried many different remedies. Once they had him smoke a cigar, and another time they made him drink strong black coffee. They tried doctors, too. Teedie wrote in his diary in Paris: "I was rubbed so hard on the chest this morning that the blood came out." Nothing helped him for long.

Still, their father hustled the children through nine countries, endlessly enthusiastic about museums, battlefields, famous buildings, gardens, parks, and operas. Despite his health problems, Teedie caught some of this enthusiasm. He wrote in his diary that he enjoyed hiking in France, visiting a natural history museum in Austria, playing ball with new friends in Rome, and touring Italian art galleries.

The Roosevelts returned to the United States in May 1870, and Teedie was soon hard at work on his museum. Although he had over one thousand items, he wanted more. He spread the word in the neighborhood that he would pay ten cents for a field mouse and thirty-five cents for a family of mice. He added that he would also buy any other creature that could swim, run, fly, or crawl. Soon Teedie's treasures were running, flying, and crawling in every room of the Roosevelt home. The family laundress threatened to leave when she found three turtles tied to the legs of her washtub.

Teedie's boyhood sketches of animals.

In his journal, Teedie recorded both the common and scientific names of the animals and birds he studied. He seemed to have no problem writing "salamander (*Diemictylus iridescens*)"; "hamster mouse (*Hesperomys myoides*)"; "bald-headed eagle (*Halietus leucocephalus*)." However, he often misspelled more familiar words: "ofserv-a-tion" for observation; "beetlles" for beetles; "yoused" for used.

Unfortunately, he still suffered from exhausting asthma attacks. In the fall of 1870, Theodore Roosevelt, Sr., once again sought medical advice. The doctors were not optimistic. They said that the mere act of breathing put a strain on Teedie's heart. Theodore, Sr., concluded then that there was only one answer.

"Theodore, you have the mind but you have not the body, and without the help of the body the mind cannot go as far as it should. You must *make* your body."

Teedie accepted the challenge. "I will make my body," he promised.

Teedie began exercising, first at Wood's Gymnasium and then in a gymnasium that his father built on the second-floor porch of their house. There he swung chest weights, pulled himself up on horizontal bars, and pounded away on a punching bag. He spent long hours alone, pushing and pulling and stretching, seen only by peacocks and magpies which lived in a garden facing the porch.

He experienced fewer asthma attacks, and he began to feel that he had, indeed, made his body. By the next summer, just before his thirteenth birthday, he enjoyed the family vacation in the country as he never had before. He ran and hiked and played games. He even went swimming in some icy rapids—and said he enjoyed it. One day he hiked up and down a mountain, and then, just for the fun of it, made the trip up and down again.

That fall, he added heavier weights to his chest machine, and he added hours to his schedule of body-building. The harder he worked, the stronger he became. His training successes showed Teedie the benefits of what he was later to call the "strenuous life."

Teedie's days were never long enough to satisfy him. Besides working out, he wanted to read more and to learn more. One of his friends called him "the most studious little brute I ever knew in my life." Private tutors taught him English, French, German, Latin, and taxidermy, the art of preparing, stuffing, and mounting the skins of dead animals.

He mounted skins so eagerly that he soon ran out of animals. His father bought him a breech-loading gun, which Teedie described as "an excellent gun for a clumsy and often absent-minded boy."

But something was wrong. Teedie never hit anything. Although his friends often came home loaded with birds, rabbits, and other small animals, Teedie always returned empty-handed. He solved the mystery himself when his friends stopped one day to read a billboard in the distance. He described the scene in his diary: "Not only was I unable to read the sign, but I could not even see the letters. I spoke of this to my father, and soon afterwards, got my first pair of spectacles." Suddenly Teedie lived in a new world of color, details, shapes, and movements.

He felt confident now, believing that the glasses and the bodybuilding were the beginning of a new life for him.

Although he had improved his health and stamina, he was still physically far behind other youngsters of his age. He discovered this in the summer of 1872, when he was sent off by himself to the country to recuperate from an asthma attack. His companions in the stagecoach were about his age. They teased and bullied him. At first, Teedie tried to fight back, but he was ridiculously weak in comparison.

Two years of body-building had not prepared him to defend himself. He resolved then to spend more time on body-building and to learn self-defense.

Chapter 3
Studies and Romance

Theodore Roosevelt, Sr., planned another trip. Beginning in October 1872, the family would travel in the Middle East for a year. This time Teedie was excited. With his body now strong enough for long hikes, his glasses, and his growing knowledge of animals and taxidermy, he looked forward to hunting for specimens in a foreign land. He prepared his list for packing: ammunition; scalpel, forceps, and scissors for dissecting; arsenic for preserving; lots of paper for recording observations; pink labels for identification of specimens.

By December, the Roosevelts were living in a houseboat, cruising up the Nile River from Cairo, Egypt.

As he had planned, Teedie spent hours stalking, shooting, and mounting specimens of owls, sparrows, ducks, cranes, and other birds. He spent many mornings riding off on a donkey, looking for birds and animals to add to his collection. His family was not as thrilled as he was. His brother, Ellie, who had to room with him, was disgusted to find bloody animal intestines in their bathroom basin. His sister Conie complained, "When he does come into the room, you always hear the words 'bird' and 'skin.' " His mother, the delicate Mittie who always wore exquisite white

Roosevelt dressed for rowing at Harvard.

silk or muslin dresses, probably shuddered when Teedie came near with his clothes and body reeking of chemicals and stained with ink. Still, Teedie triumphantly preserved over two hundred specimens.

Theodore Roosevelt, Sr., insisted that his children continue their studies on this trip. He sent Teedie, Ellie, and Conie to live with a German family in Dresden for the summer of 1873 to study language, history, and other subjects. Only Bamie was free to spend the summer with Mittie in visits to health spas and in shopping trips to London and Paris. Theodore, Sr., returned to America. Teedie studied about eight hours a day. He wrote in his diary, "I like it for I really feel that I am making considerable progress."

His biggest problem was continuing with his taxidermy, for his German hosts refused to let him use arsenic. Once they threw his mice out the window. Still he managed to add to his collection of reptiles, hedgehogs, and other small animals.

Thoughts of animals filled his mind. When he wrote home about having the mumps, he described himself as an old woodchuck with his cheeks filled with nuts. When asthma attacks left him struggling for breath, he compared himself to a hippopotamus.

Teedie's cousins John and Maud Elliott (Mittie's brother's children) were visiting in Dresden at the same time. The five cousins met every Sunday afternoon to read original stories and poems. In front of adults, they called this group the Dresden Literary American Club. Their secret name was WANA (We Are No Asses).

Fifteen-year-old Teedie arrived back in New York in November 1873. Immediately, he started studying for Harvard College entrance exams to be held in the summer of 1875. He was already strong in science, history, geography, and modern language. His father hired a new tutor to help him with math, Latin, and Greek. Teedie set up a study schedule of six to eight hours daily, five days a week.

The WANA Club in Dresden, July 1873. From left to right: Teedie, Elliott, Cousin Maud Elliott, Corinne, Cousin John Elliott.

Theodore Roosevelt, Sr., now a multimillionaire, built a gym on the top floor of their New York City mansion. He also rented a plantation-style home on Oyster Bay, Long Island. There the children swam, fished, and played in the woods.

Theodore guided his children both by words and by example. "I always believe in showing affection by doing what will please the one we love, not by talking," he said. He encouraged his children to be happy. "Man was never intended to be an oyster." Teedie wanted to be just like his father.

In the water and woods around Oyster Bay, Teedie found dozens of new specimens for his museum. He wrote detailed observations in his notebooks. The winter wren fascinated him: "Rather common in the dense woods, but rarely seen. It is often heard, however, for it possesses a gushing, ringing sound, wonderfully loud for so small a creature."

On his seventeenth birthday, Teedie proudly recorded that he weighed one hundred twenty-four pounds; stood five feet, eight inches tall; had a chest measurement of twenty-four inches; and sported new fuzzy side whiskers. In addition to body-building exercises, he rowed and swam, and he competed with his cousins in running and jumping.

His sense of humor grew, too. One friend said she dreaded sitting next to him at formal dinner parties because he made her laugh so hard that she became embarrassed.

He spent a lot of time with Edith Kermit Carow, daughter of family friends. She may have been his first real girlfriend.

Theodore, as he now wanted to be called, entered Harvard in the fall of 1876. He soon gained a reputation for his arrogant mannerisms in class. He did not hesitate to interrupt his professors to ask questions or to complain that their lectures were unclear or misleading. One professor scolded him: "See here, Roosevelt, let me talk. *I'm* running this course."

Staff members of the Harvard Advocate. *Roosevelt is on the right in the back row.*

Study and classes filled most of his time from nine in the morning until four-thirty in the afternoon, and then he studied again after dinner until eleven o'clock. Somehow he also squeezed in boxing, wrestling, body-building, dancing classes, teaching in Sunday school, rowing, and, of course, adding to his collections. He also wrote for the Harvard *Advocate*. Several classmates admitted later that they were confused by Theodore's boundless energy. One wondered if "he is the real thing or only a bundle of eccentricities which he appears."

Everyone on campus knew that Theodore loved to talk. Because he read so much, he could discuss many different subjects—boxing, bird-watching, Abraham Lincoln, the Dead Sea—almost anything at all. "Reading with me is a disease," he said. He later explained how he remembered most of what he read. "As I talked, the pages of the book came before my eyes."

He had a slight stammer and a high-pitched voice. When he was excited, words spluttered out of his mouth faster than his voice could shape them. Some acquaintances called him peculiar or even crazy because of the way he spoke. Everyone called him interesting.

Of course, he set up a laboratory in his rented room. Salamanders, snakes, lobsters, and other small animals lived there for short periods until he found time to add them to his permanent collection. One day a huge tortoise escaped and was found by Theodore's landlady, Mrs. Richards. Theodore had to use all his charm to persuade her to let him continue to room there.

In the summer of 1877, Theodore published his first "book"—a short pamphlet called *The Summer Birds of the Adirondacks*. In this book, he described the appearance and songs of ninety-seven species of the area.

Before he went back to Harvard for his second year in 1877, Theodore had a long talk with his father about his studies and his career. Theodore's father had hoped that he would become a businessman, but Theodore preferred working outdoors to being in an office, and he preferred zoology to accounting courses. They agreed that he should follow his heart and become a natural scientist although this meant that he would never be a wealthy man.

With that decision made, Theodore spent the rest of the summer and his semester breaks on hunting, fishing, and hiking trips. Everywhere he went, he made scientific notes and illustrations of the birds and animals he saw. His asthma rarely bothered him, and he was often the strongest and fastest hiker in his group.

When his father died suddenly of cancer in February 1878, young Theodore grieved, "I often feel badly that such a wonderful man as Father should have had a son of so little worth as I am." He set himself a goal: "How I wish I could ever do something to keep up his name!"

Despite his grief, Theodore Roosevelt became more outgoing in his third year at Harvard. His fellow students appreciated his ever-inquisitive mind and his intensity about everything from sports to studies. He joined some college clubs with high social status, and he attended parties. Theodore enjoyed dancing although one of his partners said, "He danced just as you'd expect him to dance if you knew him —he hopped."

As his social life grew, so did his concern about his looks. He waxed his mustache, and he wore his glasses on a black silk cord. Perhaps unconsciously, he began to dress as his father had with shiny silk ties, cameo pins, and even a silk hat. He spent lavishly. In his last two years in college, he spent $2,400 on clothes and club dues. In those times, the average American family could live on about $400 a year.

His attitude toward his studies changed, also. He was disappointed in zoology and botany, where he was required to spend his time in laboratories with microscopes and notebooks and textbooks. He missed his long days outdoors with live animals and his hunting, dissecting, and mounting. He began to rethink his career plans. Did he want to spend the rest of his life in laboratories?

In the fall of 1878, he met Alice Hathaway Lee, a tall blond beauty. After their third meeting, Theodore resolved to marry her. He declared, "I had never before cared. . . a snap of my finger for any girl."

That winter and spring, Theodore often woke at five o'clock and studied for about nine hours. Then he mounted his horse, Lightfoot, to head for Chestnut Hill where Alice lived. They danced and tobogganed and walked and talked.

Theodore disliked his science courses. Besides, Alice did not share his love of specimens and experiments. He began to consider a career in politics or law.

When they met again in the fall of 1879, after a summer apart, Alice showed little interest in Theodore. Although puzzled and deeply disappointed, Theodore continued to believe that they would marry.

To take his mind off this problem, he started to write a book, *The Naval War of 1812*. As a child he had been fascinated with stories told by his maternal uncle, James Bulloch, an officer in the Confederate navy. His study of history increased this interest. His book would focus on the role of the navy in the War of 1812 between the British and the new American nation.

Suddenly Alice Lee changed her mind about Theodore again. The day after Christmas in 1879, they resumed the courtship. Theodore proposed marriage, and Alice accepted. He wrote in his diary, "How she, so pure and sweet and beautiful can think of marrying me I can not understand, but I praise and thank God it is so."

More than romance was on Theodore's mind in the spring of 1880. Before his graduation that June, he was required to write a very long essay called a dissertation. He urged that women be given the right to vote in his paper entitled "The Practicality of Giving Men and Women Equal Rights."

Life seemed perfect for Theodore. He graduated twenty-first in a class of one hundred seventy-seven. He had an excellent academic record, a place in high society, a fair degree of wealth, and even a record as a lightweight college boxer. He was engaged to be married to the girl of his dreams.

He told no one, not even Alice, of his visit to a doctor three months before graduation. The doctor told him that his heart had been seriously damaged by years of asthma attacks and overexertion. He declared that Theodore must live a quiet life or he could not expect to live a long one.

Alice Lee (about 1878–1880).

Perhaps he did not believe the doctor. Perhaps he was instinctively following his father's model of living life to the fullest. For whatever reason, he immediately launched a vigorous routine of tennis, hiking, boating, and swimming at Oyster Bay. In August 1880, he took a hunting trip in the Midwest with his brother, Elliott. When he returned, he bragged that he had been bitten by a snake, thrown headfirst out of a wagon, and soaked and then nearly frozen in rainstorms.

Theodore was proving the doctor wrong.

*At Oyster Bay (about 1878). Seated from left to right are
Theodore, Corinne, Anna, and Elliott. Alice is standing.*

Chapter 4
"Into the Hurly-Burly"

On October 27, 1880, Theodore's twenty-second birthday, he and nineteen-year-old Alice were married. The newlyweds quickly became part of New York's high society. They visited frequently in the elegant homes of the Astors and the Vanderbilts, and they entertained just as lavishly in their own home furnished with Tiffany glass and scratchy horsehair furniture.

Theodore's father had left him one hundred twenty-five thousand dollars. By investing this money and receiving the interest, he had a yearly income of eight thousand dollars. "I had enough to get bread," he said. "What I had to do, if I wanted butter and jam, was to provide the butter and jam." Although he would work, money-making would not have to be his chief goal in life.

Theodore entered Columbia Law School where he was again a questioning and eager student. As he learned more about laws and government, he kept in mind his father's teaching that every individual has a duty to serve his fellow man. Through his studies he became aware of the political climate of the nation, of New York State, and especially of New York City.

Immigrants on board a ship to America.

That political climate was based on the idea of freedom. In America at that time, businesses and individuals were free to act with little or no government regulation. John D. Rockefeller built a fortune in the oil business by driving out competitors against his firm, the Standard Oil Company. Employers who hired immigrants (over three million arrived between 1865 and 1875) showed little concern for safe working conditions or fair wages. Landlords rented out filthy rooms in dangerous, decaying tenements.

Serious problems existed in industry. In August 1882, a Senate Committee on Education and Labor investigated labor-management relations in the country. They found that workers in a carriage factory had to ask permission to get a drink of water since the faucets were locked. Drivers of the horse-railroads in New York City were required to stand the entire fourteen hours of their workday. Women making cigars in shops were required to sit back-to-back and to remain silent throughout the day. A physician testified that factory workers were physically small because they are "shut up all day long in the noise and in the high temperature of these mills."

The people to whom the factory workers might complain—building inspectors, judges, city officials—were often dependent on the "spoils system" for their jobs. Under the spoils system, the politicians who won elections appointed as officials citizens who had supported them. Competence, experience, and honesty were less important job qualifications than party loyalty.

When a new party came into power, the winners appointed new officials, again with little reference to competence or honesty.

Theodore knew about these political rewards, also called *patronage,* firsthand. In 1877, the New York State Senate failed to approve his father's nomination for an important job, the post of collector of customs for the Port of New York. The rejection was based on party politics, not on Theodore Roosevelt, Sr.'s ability to do the job.

Theodore set a new challenge for himself. He would become active in government so that he would have the power to fight corruption and ensure that each citizen could rise according to his ability.

Theodore chose to join the Republican party, as his father had. He explained his choice: "A young man of my bringing-up and convictions could join only the Republican party." This was, in part, because during the Civil War, the Republicans had stood for a united country. Also, the leading Democrats in New York State—a group called Tammany Hall after the name of their meeting place—were known to be politically corrupt. While dominating New York City government, Tammany members stole millions of dollars.

Republicans were active on two levels. Prominent lawyers and businessmen contributed money to candidates who would help them most in their businesses and law practices. Workingmen proposed names of likely candidates, walked the streets to encourage votes for their candidates, and tried to influence appointments by the mayor and other officials. The second group, the Republican Club, was the one Theodore chose to work with. He wrote, "The man who, in the long run, will count for most in bettering municipal life is the man who actually steps down into the hurly-burly." Theodore Roosevelt started on the bottom rung of the political ladder.

At first the Republican Club members scoffed when they heard Roosevelt's patent leather shoes on the wooden stairs. They stared as he bounded into the drab room furnished with rough benches and spittoons. Often dressed in elegant evening clothes for an engagement later that night, he was a startling contrast to the others, who were dressed in their working clothes as saloon keepers, horsecar conductors, and factory workers. Finally he won their respect because, he said, "I went there often enough to have the men get accustomed to me and for me to get accustomed to them." He did not expect special privileges because of his wealth and position, nor did he expect to be scorned for being different.

Theodore's society friends never did accept the fact that he met with these men, whom they considered "rough, brutal, and unpleasant." However, most of his family and his father's friends cheered for him, believing him to be an excellent model of integrity for their class.

He rose fast. By March of 1881, he was elected to the executive committee of the Young Republicans. That was the year that Republican president James Garfield was assassinated, and Vice-President Chester Arthur became president.

By the fall of 1881, Theodore admitted to himself that he was losing interest in law school. In fact, he disapproved of what he was learning—that wealth serves the wealthy, law serves lawyers, and business serves businessmen. He had wider goals in mind for his life. He would become a participant in government so that he could bring about reform. Among his father's letters which he kept near was one that said, "We cannot stand so corrupt a government for any great length of time."

As usual, Theodore worked on several projects at once. He kept working on his naval history, mastering complicated details of ship construction and sea battles as he went along. The book was published in May 1882 and praised by civilians and military people alike.

His love of natural history continued. He offered some of his collection of specimens and notes to the Smithsonian Institution in Washington, D.C. The secretary of the Institution praised the careful preservation and the detailed notes. In just one year, Theodore sent more than six hundred specimens from as far away as Egypt and as close as the Adirondack Mountains in New York State.

In October 1881, the day after his twenty-third birthday, Theodore Roosevelt ran for state assemblyman (representative) from New York's

Twenty-First District. He wrote in his autobiography: "There was no real party division on most of the things that were of concern." However, he promised to vote "strong Republican on State [federal] matters, but independent on local and municipal affairs." He declared that he would not let party loyalty interfere with his fight against corruption wherever he found it. He reported in his diary, "I was triumphantly elected." And triumphantly he served.

John Walsh, a fellow legislator, described the first day that Roosevelt entered the Assembly chambers in Albany, New York:

> His hair was parted in the center, and he had sideburns. He wore a single eye-glass with a gold chain over his ear. He had on a cutaway coat...the ends of its tails almost reached the tips of his shoes. He carried a gold-headed cane in one hand, a silk hat in the other...
>
> "Who's the dude?" I asked another member.

One reporter described Roosevelt's behavior on the Assembly floor: "He was just like a Jack coming out of the box. . . . He yelled and pounded his desk, and when they attacked him, he would fire back with all the venom imaginary."

In his autobiography, Roosevelt writes that "there were a great many thoroughly corrupt men in the Legislature, perhaps a third of the whole number." Assemblyman Roosevelt was eager to correct this situation.

Some legislators were also businessmen who took advantage of their political power to help their companies or other businessmen. This advantage was evident in a bill concerning the building of a railway terminal. These legislators could make a great deal of money by granting the building contract to special friends. They wanted to delay the progress of the bill from the Cities Committee (which Roosevelt chaired) to the full Assembly in order to have time to put through their own deals.

Before he rose to speak in favor of the bill, Roosevelt took a leg from a broken chair and laid it on the floor beside him "where I might get at it in

Roosevelt and fellow New York State assemblymen (1884).
He is standing on the right.

a hurry." He recommended that legislators send the bill to the Assembly with a request for a positive response. The men voted down his request.

Determined to get the bill onto the Assembly floor, he recommended that they send it there with a request for a negative response. Again he was voted down.

Roosevelt did not give up. "I then put the bill in my pocket and announced that I would report it anyhow. This almost precipitated a riot, especially when I explained. . . that I suspected that the men holding up all report of the bill were holding it up for purposes of blackmail."

The riot did not occur. No one can say for sure if this was because Roosevelt was in the right or because he had the chair leg ready. In the end, the bill was taken from Roosevelt's control, and it was finally passed by the whole Assembly.

Some people remembered this story when Roosevelt explained his "big stick," theory in a speech in 1901. At that time he quoted a West African proverb, "Speak softly, but carry a big stick," to explain his method for persuading people to agree with him. His big stick was the threat of force which he hoped would make that force unnecessary.

Roosevelt the reformer became famous overnight when he demanded that the legislature investigate State Supreme Court Justice T. R. Westbrook, a Republican. He believed the judge had used his position to swindle thousands of dollars for himself and his friends. Roosevelt's thorough investigation proved the charges to be true.

Reaction was mixed. The *New York Times* complimented him on his "most refreshing habit of calling men and things by their right names." Democratic and Republican politicians alike scorned him for barging into a situation that was none of his business. Republicans were particularly angry that Roosevelt had attacked a member of his own party.

Samuel Gompers, a young leader in the labor movement, asked Roosevelt to support a bill outlawing the making of cigars at home. At

Samuel Gompers in later life.

This photograph by Jacob Riis shows an immigrant family making cigars in their tenement apartment.

first, Roosevelt refused because he thought that government should not interfere with business. Gompers then took him on a tour of tenement houses where cigars were made.

Roosevelt showed that he could change his mind when proven wrong. On the tour he found whole families working day and night in dark, crowded apartments, surrounded by heaps of tobacco. In many cases, the tenements were owned by the cigar makers' employers. He promptly came out in favor of the measure. "As a matter of practical common sense," he wrote afterward, "I could not conscientiously vote for the continuation of the conditions which I saw."

Most men of Roosevelt's social class would have agreed with his first instinct, which was to ignore the situation. They believed that each man created his own wealth or poverty, and that government should not play a part. Roosevelt could proudly point to his own family as an example. His ancestors had begun their lives in the United States as pig farmers in Old Manhattan and worked their way to the wealth which Theodore and his family enjoyed.

Thus, when streetcar employees asked the legislature to create a law limiting their workday to twelve hours, Roosevelt spoke against the bill. He believed that business conditions, not legislation, should determine working hours.

At the end of his first six-month term in the legislature, Roosevelt looked forward to another term. In the fall of 1882, he was easily reelected.

Early in 1883, New York's Democratic governor, Grover Cleveland, asked Roosevelt to help abolish the spoils system. Cleveland had chosen the right man. Always a strong competitor himself, Roosevelt was eager to work against forces which prevented a man from using his intelligence and hard work to get ahead. His bill, known as a *civil service reform* measure, required that ten percent of all government (civil service) jobs be filled through competitive written tests. The bill, which was passed in May 1883, also protected a government employee from being fired for any reason except incompetence. Roosevelt's work did not end the spoils system, but he knew that a small start is better than no progress at all.

In all his reform measures, Roosevelt was true to the ideals he had learned from his father. He believed that each man had to create his own future. The state was responsible for ensuring equal opportunity. The citizen himself was responsible for accepting the challenge.

Although he was busier than ever, he traveled from Albany every weekend to be with Alice. He wrote in his diary: "I can imagine nothing more happy in life than an evening spent in my cozy sitting room . . . with my own dainty mistress."

Perhaps his colleagues in the Assembly chambers would not have recognized him at home. In Albany, he became louder and more boisterous to the point of being rude. Newspaper reporters followed him around because he often made the kind of statement that readers love. He called one newspaper owner an "arch thief," and he described a Democratic assemblyman as an "altogether unnecessary and impossible statesman." He spoke of many of his fellow legislators as "men whose intentions are excellent, but whose intellects are foggy."

At the end of the legislative session in the spring of 1883, Roosevelt planned a trip to the Bad Lands of the Dakota Territory. He was determined to shoot a buffalo. "I am fond of politics," he confided, "but fonder still of a little big game hunting." In September he was on his way to the West, leaving Alice, who was then pregnant.

First he had to prove himself to the men who would help him in his hunting. These cowboys could not easily accept the Eastern "dude" with his fancy alligator boots, silver spurs, tooled leather belt, and Colt revolver with the handle elaborately engraved with scrolls and geometric

Roosevelt as a cowboy in the Bad Lands of North Dakota.

patterns. Also, "when I went among strangers," he wrote in his auto-biography, "I always had to spend twenty-four hours living down the fact that I wore spectacles."

The cowboys soon learned that appearance did not define this man. One night in a hotel, a customer waved a pistol and announced, "Four Eyes is going to treat." When Roosevelt pretended not to hear, the man came closer to his table. Roosevelt hit him in the jaw, knocking him to the floor. After that, Theodore was left in peace.

Roosevelt spent the first week in the Bad Lands riding through drizzles and downpours, up slippery slopes and across rolling prairie, wet through to his skin and covered with sticky mud. He saw only antelopes. He refused to return to camp until the second week, when he finally shot a buffalo.

He also rode in the roundups. There were no fences in the West, so cowboys had to ride out regularly to bring back cows which had strayed and to brand newborn calves. These roundups often lasted for three and four days. During this time, the men stopped only long enough to bring back the lost cows and newborns and to change horses. Then they charged out onto the plains again. Roosevelt was leading a strenuous life—and fully enjoying it.

With his typical enthusiasm for new projects, Roosevelt soon spent fourteen thousand dollars to buy and stock a cattle ranch, the Maltese Cross, in what is now North Dakota. (The next year, he spent twenty-six thousand to buy one thousand more cattle and another ranch, the Elkhorn.) In these years, he was making about thirteen thousand a year, including the money he inherited from his father. Family members questioned his extravagance. He admitted that his expenditures "certainly have been very heavy," but he showed little concern. Roosevelt was not, nor did he want to be, a thrifty man. In his ranch investments, he yielded to his love of the outdoors, of adventure, and of the lifestyle of the West.

Delighted that he owned a piece of the West, Roosevelt returned to New York in the fall of 1883 for his third term as legislator. He campaigned to become Speaker of the House, the lawmaker who would preside over the Assembly meetings. He lost the election, but he quickly overcame his disappointment and returned to working up to fourteen hours a day. He soon issued three new bills against government corruption in New York City and New York State.

On February 13, 1884, he received a telegram announcing the birth of a baby daughter the night before. A few hours later, he received another telegram. Both Alice and his mother were seriously ill.

He rushed home to New York City, where the women lived together. He arrived shortly before midnight to find Alice already in a coma, dying of kidney failure. Two hours later, he learned that his mother was also near death. He spent one hour with her before she died of typhoid fever at three o'clock that morning.

In agonized bewilderment, he rushed back to Alice. At two o'clock that afternoon, she died.

His grief was too great to express. The twenty-five-year-old widower marked a large cross in his diary on that night and wrote: "The light has gone out of my life." He remained stunned throughout the funeral and the christening of Baby Alice Lee on February 17, 1884. Feeling that he could not care for Alice on his own, he accepted Bamie's offer to be responsible for the child.

The next day he returned to Albany, saying, "There is nothing left for me except to try to so live as not to dishonor the memory of those I loved who have gone before me."

"Held Up by Buffalo," a painting by N. H. Trotter (about 1880).

Chapter 5
At Home on the Range

Roosevelt tried to relieve his grief with work. He investigated corruption in the New York City police department, where jobs were bought and sold. He complained about the city prisons, where inmates had to pay for clean beds and decent food. He proposed additional funding for the Bill for the Benefit of Colored Orphans. He wrote dozens of reports—one fifteen thousand words long—on his investigation of illegal practices in the liquor business.

Other investigations showed Roosevelt that many government clerks were collecting double fees for their work. Although they received salaries, they demanded that citizens pay them for services. Some people even set up offices and charged for services that should have been free. A tax assessor admitted that he imposed taxes by "intuition," and that he was responsible to no one.

In his three terms in the legislature, Roosevelt became known as a man of integrity, both in his own dealings and in his judgments of others. He initiated nine reform bills, seven of which were passed. Among the most important ones were bills limiting the power of city and state legislators to buy and sell government jobs. Common citizens cheered him as a legislator who attacked corruption wherever he found it, even if it involved a fellow party member.

In June 1884, Roosevelt attended the Republican National Convention in Chicago. He supported Vermont senator George Edmunds as presidential nominee despite pleas from fellow Republicans to support either Maine congressman James Blaine or the incumbent president, Chester Arthur. His vigorous opposition to his party caught the attention of reporters. Soon the name of Theodore Roosevelt was known throughout the country.

When Blaine won the nomination, reporters asked Roosevelt if he would support a man whom he had criticized throughout the convention. Apparently unsure about whether to remain loyal to his principles or to the party, he answered, "It is a subject I do not care to talk about." However, in the fall, he did support Blaine.

Later in June, he refused the nomination for a fourth term in the Assembly saying, "I think I shall spend the next two or three years in making shooting trips, either in the Far West or in the Northern Woods and there will be plenty of work to do writing."

After a few weeks in the Bad Lands, he wrote in his diary: "I have been having a glorious time here, and am well hardened now. . . . The country is growing on me, more and more. . . and as I own six or eight horses I have a fresh one every day and ride on a lope all day long."

During 1885 and 1886, he wrote extensively. He worked on *Hunting Trips of a Ranchman*, describing his delight in living in the West, and a biography, the *Life of Thomas Hart Benton*, about a senator and champion of the Westward movement. His earlier book, *The Naval War of 1812*, remained popular.

Life in the West—exciting, risky, and challenging—was well suited to Theodore Roosevelt's personality. From 1860 to the end of the century, one hundred seventy thousand miles of railroad track were laid. This

Laying railroad track in Montana (1887).

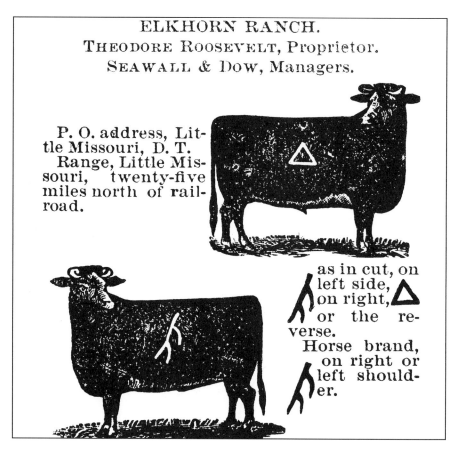

ELKHORN RANCH.
THEODORE ROOSEVELT, Proprietor.
SEAWALL & DOW, Managers.

P. O. address, Little Missouri, D. T.
Range, Little Missouri, twenty-five miles north of railroad.

as in cut, on left side, on right, or the reverse.
Horse brand, on right or left shoulder.

Cattle brands from the Elkhorn Ranch.

project brought many workers to the West. Ranchers could now ship their cattle to meat-packing plants in the East. They hired thousands of cowboys to oversee the herds, which roamed at will in this land without fences. Because buffaloes were considered obstacles to growth and travel, hundreds of thousands of them were killed. Sometimes, for fun, travelers shot them from moving trains. Cities, towns, and simple overnight stops were built, and government and law could not keep up with this growth. Conflict increased between the land-hungry settlers and the Native Americans. This was the era of the "Wild West," where each man carried a gun and sought his own justice.

Roosevelt with the two ranch foremen who helped capture the boat thieves.

Once Theodore sought justice for himself. Thieves stole a boat he had tied near his camp on the Little Missouri River. The only clue to the theft was one red mitten left at the scene. Roosevelt and two ranch foremen built a scow and began poling through the icy winter water. Four days later, they surprised the thieves. Many Westerners would have hung the thieves immediately. Roosevelt and his companions spent the next eight days taking their prisoners to the nearest jail.

Other adventures included trips to collect animal specimens to take back East. The party traveled in a ranch wagon carrying essential food like flour, bacon, coffee, sugar, and salt. On each trip, Roosevelt added to his collection of animal heads which now included elk, Rocky Mountain goat, grizzly bear, bighorn, and caribou.

Around this time, he and some fellow hunters began to consider another aspect of hunting. Naturalist George Grinnell later said, "We regretted the unnecessary destruction of game animals, but we did not know all it meant."

Roosevelt thought that the Western pioneers were different both from their European ancestors and from the Native Americans. He believed that the harsh living conditions of the West had created a unique group of people—more hard-working, independent, courageous, and ready to accept challenges than any people before them.

He concluded that his own Western experiences had given him these "new American" qualities. Later, he declared that without this background, he might never have become president. "I owe more than I can ever express to the West," he said.

Like many other Americans, however, he believed that the Indians had no ownership rights to land since they traveled over wide areas and did not build settlements. When Indians attacked whites who were claiming the land for themselves, Roosevelt and others called the Indians "troublesome" and "bloodthirsty."

Despite his attachment to the West, he did not neglect little Alice, who was well and happy with Bamie. Roosevelt returned to New York frequently to visit her. He also kept contact with his publishers during these visits.

These trips kept him aware of the conflict that was growing between workers and employers throughout the country. Workers were rebelling against low wages, long hours, and poor working conditions. John D. Rockefeller of the Standard Oil Company spoke for many business leaders, justifying their treatment of workers. "The growth of large business is merely a survival of the fittest...a law of nature and of God," he explained.

Workers who rebelled were easily replaced, often with others who

An artist's drawing of the bomb exploding at the Haymarket rally.

accepted even lower wages, longer hours, and worse conditions. Some workers accepted any job, not daring to complain. Some tried to organize unions to improve conditions.

The labor conflict heightened. On May 1, 1886, workers in Chicago held a large and peaceful demonstration for an eight-hour workday. Two days later, Chicago police were called in to the McCormick Harvester plant, where strikers and strikebreakers were fighting. One worker was killed, and others were wounded. The next day, as police tried to break up a workers' rally in Haymarket Square in Chicago, someone threw a bomb. Historians disagree on the number of casualties, but at least one policeman (and perhaps as many as eight) was killed. Seven strike leaders were later sentenced to death for the killings although the courts did not prove them guilty.

A reconstruction of Roosevelt's cabin at his Maltese Cross Ranch.

Roosevelt took sides against the striking workers, accusing them of asking for too much. Like his father and the other wealthy men he had known, Roosevelt believed that no man should ask for help. Instead, he should pull himself up by his own bootstraps. Roosevelt declared that his own ranch hands also disapproved of the Chicago workers' actions. "I believe nothing would give them [my workers] greater pleasure than a chance with their rifles at one of the mobs."

By the summer of 1886, Roosevelt decided that he could no longer remain out West, removed from the problems of the world.

His two years in the West had refreshed him in body and spirit. He had met physical challenges which left him both exhausted and victorious. He had come to respect men of very different backgrounds, and they respected him.

Besides, he had been courting Edith Carow, his childhood friend, on his trips to New York and by mail. She had agreed to marriage. They both wanted Alice to live with them. With these matters settled, Roosevelt was ready to return to family life and responsibility in the East.

Chapter 6
An Election Lost,
An Appointment Earned

When Roosevelt arrived in New York in the fall of 1886, he found the Republicans determined that he run for mayor. He yielded to party pressure although he said he knew that it was "a perfectly hopeless contest" in a three-way race. Nevertheless, he campaigned eighteen hours a day, often attending several meetings each night.

Some newspaper editors and reporters cheered for him. On October 22, they headlined, "Piping Hot—Roosevelt Busy as a Beaver"; on October 24, the headline was "The Roosevelt Tidal Wave—Growing Strength of the Candidate"; on October 27, it was "All Solid for Roosevelt." But politicians were saying that Roosevelt was too young, too much of a reformer, and too quick to shout out his opinion. Final returns gave him only sixty thousand votes against the winner's ninety thousand.

On December 2, 1886, he sailed to England where he married Edith Carow. After a fifteen-week honeymoon, the newlyweds moved into a house that he had begun for Alice at Oyster Bay. Called Sagamore Hill

Roosevelt (about 1884).

Sagamore Hill.

(after a local Indian chief), the house had twenty-eight rooms. Although Bamie wanted to keep Alice, she yielded to Edith's insistence that Theodore's three-year-old daughter belonged with her father and her new stepmother.

Finances were a problem. Although Roosevelt had a small income from the money his father had left him, he had no job, and expenses at Sagamore Hill were high. In addition, news from the ranch was not good.

In 1886–1887, the worst winter in frontier history, the temperature fell to more than forty degrees below zero, and three to four feet of snow covered the prairies where the cattle had been left to graze. Some cattle froze to death from the stinging wind and cold, and their bodies were found with their hooves locked in ice. Others simply starved to death.

In the March thaw, floods primed with melting snow brought the carcasses of tens of thousands of cattle rushing over the prairies and into the valleys.

Roosevelt had lost two-thirds of his cattle. He sold his property in the Bad Lands at a loss of about seventy thousand dollars. To support his family, he turned again to writing. In only three months in 1887, he researched and wrote a biography of Gouverneur Morris, a statesman during the American Revolutionary period. That same year, his biography of Benton was published.

The first baby born to Theodore and Edith was a boy, in September 1887. The child was named Theodore Roosevelt, Jr. The proud father immediately began signing his own name, Theodore Roosevelt, Sr.

On a five-week trip to the West in the fall of 1887, Roosevelt discovered a serious problem. The very existence of animals there was threatened by the recent Westward movement of thousands of people, the devastation created by the weather of the previous winter, and years of unregulated hunting and trapping.

In December, Roosevelt along with George Grinnell and ten other men founded the [Daniel] Boone and [Davy] Crockett Club. They dedicated this first conservationist club in the country to the preservation of open land as "nurseries and reservations for woodland creatures which else would die out before the march of settlement." These men wanted to keep large areas of the West free from development. They also wanted to ensure that the Western forests would not be destroyed by lumber companies.

Members of the B and C Club led a successful fight in Congress against a large company that wanted to commercialize Yellowstone National Park in Wyoming. The company had planned to build resort hotels, a sawmill, a railroad line, and a mining operation. The club helped to establish the New York (Bronx) Zoo; suggested laws against hunting deer by forcing them into the water or blinding them with artificial lights; proposed the establishment of Glacier National Park in Montana; and published many books and articles encouraging the public to support conservation. Roosevelt wrote some of these articles, and he also edited several books.

In January 1888, Roosevelt planned a major writing project to cover the drama of American history from Daniel Boone in 1774 to Davy Crockett in 1836. He saw this as a four-to-eight-volume series titled *The Winning of the West*.

Eventually, he spent seven years writing this work. In the meantime, he earned money by writing articles on politics and on the West for popular magazines. Some of his essays were published in a book, *Essays in Practical Politics*. Six other magazine articles were published in another book, *Ranch Life and the Hunting-Trail*.

Writing seemed to offer more opportunity than politics since the Democrats were in power under President Grover Cleveland. Nevertheless, Roosevelt took time to campaign for Benjamin Harrison, the

Republican candidate for president in the fall of 1888.

Harrison won. Theodore Roosevelt, the state legislator who had fought hard and long against the spoils system, accepted a reward for his campaign help. This reward was a job that few men wanted. It paid little and seemed of minor importance. But Roosevelt gladly accepted the appointment as a Civil Service commissioner in the nation's capital.

The job would not be of minor importance for long.

Edith Carow (about 1886).

Chapter 7

"I Am the New Civil Service Commissioner"

In May 1889, Roosevelt began his new job in the beautiful city of Washington. The city was bustling with politicians, would-be politicians, clerks, and lobbyists (men who tried to persuade legislators or government officials to support or oppose various issues). The broad streets were popular meeting places for those who wanted to comment on the latest gossip. People who lived in Washington were sociable. Even President Harrison sometimes enjoyed a soda in a local drugstore.

Reformers had long criticized the patronage system for federal government jobs. When a disappointed job seeker shot President James Garfield in 1881, elimination of patronage became a popular cause. The result was the Pendleton Act of 1883, establishing the Civil Service Commission. Its three commissioners were charged with enforcing rules that banned hiring and firing for reasons other than job competence. They were also to ensure that at least one-tenth of government jobs were filled by competitive tests.

Until Roosevelt arrived, the Civil Service Commission in Washington

This cartoon shows Commissioner Roosevelt "taming" the spoils system.

was a friendly office where days passed quietly. Because they owed their own jobs to patronage, neither the commissioners nor the workers were eager to enforce the regulations.

Workers in that office must have been shocked on the morning of May 13, 1889, when Theodore Roosevelt bounded into the offices shouting, "I am the new Civil Service commissioner, Theodore Roosevelt of New York. Have you a telephone?"

After learning the hiring and firing rules in double-quick time, he mailed hundreds of letters warning officials that they were to follow these rules strictly.

His "big stick" was his eagerness to tell the real story to the public. In May, he called for the dismissal of customs officials who had sold advance information on an entrance exam for fifty dollars. He issued press releases revealing that thousands of newspaper editors who had supported Harrison had left their papers to accept jobs in government service. His speeches and reports fascinated average Americans who had never even heard of the Civil Service Commission. They began to look forward to new reports of Roosevelt's latest quarrels, accusations, and outbursts.

Theodore and Edith had decided that Edith, pregnant again, should stay at Oyster Bay. There she worried about her stepdaughter. She wrote to Theodore, "Alice needs someone to laugh and romp with her instead of a sober and staid person like me." She added, "My darling, you are all the world to me. I am not myself when you are away."

Kermit, the Roosevelts' second son, was born on October 10. Roosevelt spent two weeks at Oyster Bay, helping Edith and enjoying his growing family.

In the spring of 1890, Roosevelt's major target was the Post Office Department. In the year after Harrison's election, thirty thousand Democratic postmasters were fired, and thirty thousand Republicans took their places. The postmaster general who supervised these changes

Roosevelt with Ted, who is dressed in the custom of the time (1891).

Grover Cleveland, president from 1885 to 1889 and 1893 to 1897.

was John Wanamaker, a wealthy Republican who contributed heavily to his party. Roosevelt said about him, "I don't like him for two reasons. In the first place, he has a very sloppy mind, and in the next place, he does not tell the truth."

President Harrison, Wanamaker, and some congressmen urged Roosevelt to avoid publicity. Roosevelt paid no attention to them. He made no secret of the fact that he had sent a report to Congress outlining thousands of post office hiring and firing violations. Members of Congress complained and quarreled and worried about the report. Finally they were forced to admit publicly that Roosevelt was right. Soon, all over America, citizens were talking about Roosevelt, the fearless reformer.

In August 1891, Ethel Roosevelt, Theodore's second daughter, was born at Sagamore Hill. That winter, Edith brought the whole family—seven-year-old Alice, four-year-old Ted, two-year-old Kermit, and the infant—to Washington to live. The Roosevelts believed that they would return to Sagamore Hill in 1892 after the presidential election. They assumed that he would lose his job then, no matter who won. Harrison had already spoken against Roosevelt. If Democrat Grover Cleveland won, he would surely select someone from his own party for the job.

Cleveland did win the election. The new president and Roosevelt had worked well together when Cleveland was governor of New York State and Roosevelt was an assemblyman. He asked Roosevelt to remain in the job so that they could work together again.

For the next two years, Roosevelt worked with his usual vigor. He sent fiery reports to legislators, wrote five-thousand-word letters explaining his positions, kept up a persistent lobby at the White House, and continued to attack all those who opposed his demand that federal employees be hired for their merit alone.

Despite heavy political involvement, Roosevelt continued writing. He completed a history of the city of New York, which he called a "very commonplace little book." In this book, *New York*, published in 1891, he mentioned his satisfaction that immigrants were quickly becoming Americanized. In 1893, his book *The Wilderness Hunter* was published. It detailed the history of the West and described the windswept prairies, the mountains, and the endless forests as well as the birds and animals which lived there.

Roosevelt's good news in April 1894 was the birth of a fifth child, Archibald. The rest of that year was difficult for him personally. In August, after a long battle with alcoholism, Theodore's brother Elliott committed suicide. In October, Theodore regretfully turned down the Republican nomination for mayor of New York, yielding to Edith's wishes. Edith did not want her husband to become involved in a position which depended on the changeable will of the voters. Besides, she liked living in Washington.

*The Roosevelt family in 1895. From left: Theodore,
Archie, Ted, Alice, Kermit, Edith, and Ethel.*

With his rapidly growing family, lack of money was an increasing problem. The Civil Service Commission paid poorly, and Theodore had lost a lot of money on his Western ventures. In the spring of 1895, he left his civil service job. In his six years as commissioner, he had set up qualifications for twenty-six thousand jobs which had formerly been given out as favors. He had brought the principle of civil service to public attention. He had become widely known as a reformer, a government official of integrity, and a man who could bring about change.

Now Roosevelt was ready for a new challenge. In spite of Edith's desire to remain in Washington, Theodore accepted eagerly when Mayor William Strong of New York City offered him a job as one of four police commissioners.

Chapter 8
Taking Charge in New York City and Washington

Roosevelt started his new job with the same kind of enthusiasm he had shown in all his undertakings. One reporter described his first day at work at the police headquarters on Mulberry Street: "Running up the stairs . . . he waved us reporters to follow. . . . still running, he asked questions: 'Where are our offices? Where is the Board Room? What do we do first?' . . . [he] had himself elected President [of the police commission]."

Roosevelt needed all this energy. The New York Police Department was infested with corruption, beginning at the top with Police Chief Byrnes and extending down to the newest policeman. Many employees bought their jobs from the supervisor on the level above them. Rumor said that it cost three hundred dollars to become a patrolman and twelve thousand to become a police captain. To make up for the money they paid for their jobs, the new policemen charged fees for their work. They charged store owners for protection against thieves. They charged owners of gambling houses, which were illegal, for protection against police raids. And they charged new police department employees for jobs in the ranks below them.

Police Commissioner Roosevelt in his office.

Some city officeholders also joined the corruption. For a fee, they would exert political pressure to help someone get a job in the police department. Most of this money went into party funds.

Police officers who acquired their jobs through money or patronage were accountable to no one. They came to their posts late. They worked on other jobs during their shifts, and some did not work at all. They paid little or no attention to enforcing laws.

Police Chief Byrnes warned Roosevelt not to tamper with the system. Roosevelt told reporters, "I thoroughly distrust Byrnes, and cannot do any thorough work while he remains." Nine days later, Byrnes resigned.

Once again, Roosevelt used publicity as his big stick against corruption. He invited reporters to accompany him on investigations. A reporter for a leading New York newspaper, the *World*, described him: "When he asks a question, Mr. Roosevelt shoots it at the poor trembling policeman as he would shoot a bullet at a coyote...he shows a set of teeth calculated to unnerve the bravest.... His teeth are very white and almost as big as a colt's teeth.... They seem to say: 'Tell the truth to your commissioner, or he'll bite your head off.'...One thing our noble force may make up its mind to at once—it must do as Roosevelt says."

Night after night, Commissioner Roosevelt and reporter Jacob Riis prowled the streets. Often, they found police officers sleeping in out-of-the-way places, chatting on street corners, or enjoying the evening in all-night restaurants. Sometimes they didn't find the men anywhere in the assigned area. If men were absent from their posts, Roosevelt immediately wrote down their names and left orders for them to report to the precinct station the next morning.

Observers told a story of Roosevelt's actions one morning around two o'clock. Dressed in a long coat and with a hat pulled down over his eyes, he strolled down city streets with Riis, looking for policemen who were assigned to those beats. They found only one.

The owner of an all-night restaurant thought that the two strangers were up to no good. He rushed out of the store, looking for help. He shouted, "Where in thunder does that copper sleep?"

A short time later, Roosevelt and Riis found the missing patrolmen talking outside a liquor store. Roosevelt bellowed at them, "Why don't you two men patrol your posts?"

For a moment, the patrolmen were angry. Then Roosevelt introduced himself. A very short time later, they were at their posts.

"These midnight rambles are great fun," Roosevelt wrote. "My whole work brings me in contact with every class of people in New York." Honest citizens were delighted, too. They loved to hear stories of how Theodore Roosevelt found and punished policemen who were not doing their jobs. They loved pictures of Commissioner Roosevelt wearing a pink shirt and a black silk sash with tasseled ends dangling to his knees.

These must have been lonely days for Edith. Although Theodore lived with the family at Sagamore Hill, he often stayed in the city overnight. When he was home, he cycled to the Oyster Bay train station at seven-thirty in the morning to start his long workday.

Roosevelt still found time and energy for young people, as his father had done. With the help of Jacob Riis, he set up boxing clubs, saying, "The establishment of a boxing club in a tough neighborhood always tended to do away with knifing and gun-fighting."

He encountered serious problems with a state law prohibiting Sunday sales of liquor. This was an unpopular law, and both police and citizens ignored it.

In June 1895, Roosevelt instructed the police department to enforce the law. "I do not deal with public sentiment," he said. "I deal with the law. I shall not let up for one moment in my endeavor to make the police understand that no excuse will be permitted on their part when the law is not observed."

Roosevelt's motive was not a dislike of liquor, although he drank very little. He simply believed that all laws must be obeyed. He also wanted to do away with the corruption that resulted from the law. Saloons raised prices on Sundays. Police officers accepted bribes to allow Sunday sales. With both votes and money, saloon keepers paid off members of the corrupt political group, Tammany Hall, which controlled the city government.

Roosevelt kept up the campaign through the summer of 1895. All over the country, people watched with amazement. New Yorkers found humorous ways to fight the law. Since police were not allowed to search unless they saw evidence of liquor, some determined citizens took traveling bags and market baskets into the saloons, ready to hide bottles and glasses when a guard announced that a policeman was coming. Others learned to ask for their drinks in code: lemon soda meant wine; plain soda meant gin; cold tea was whiskey.

Roosevelt insisted on closing saloons as, one by one, owners were found guilty. Politicians, policemen, businessmen, and common citizens complained. Even Mayor Strong begged Roosevelt to soften his stand as November state and city elections neared.

"I shall not alter my course one handsbreadth," he answered, "even though Tammany carries the city by fifty thousand [votes]."

His prediction proved true. In the November elections, Democratic Tammany won by a large margin. Republicans blamed Roosevelt. His political future was dim despite the fact that he had won the admiration of many citizens. As a police commissioner, he had taught respect for the law, reduced corruption in the police department, set up stricter physical and intellectual requirements for entry into the police force, and lowered the crime rate in the city.

Still, he had failed the political test of loyalty, as he had done when he was assemblyman and Civil Service commissioner. Once again he had

This cartoon shows the "watchdog" police commissioner who enforced the Sunday liquor ("excise") law. The caption reads, "He's all right when you know him. But you've got to know him first."

shown fellow Republicans that he could not be trusted to defend party members and practices blindly.

He also created serious problems within the department when he proved that another commissioner, Andrew Parker, had accepted a four-hundred-dollar bribe from a job seeker. This incident led to hours of accusations, counteraccusations, and time-consuming, frustrating conflict. Finally, Mayor Strong reluctantly dismissed Parker, whom he had appointed, on charges of neglect of duty.

Asserting that he found police work "grimy," Roosevelt looked for a new challenge. He saw a possibility in the nomination of William McKinley for president in June 1896. Throughout the fall, while continuing his police work, Roosevelt campaigned vigorously for McKinley.

For a few months, he relaxed by spending more time with his family. Edith said that in one weekend, Theodore "played bear so hard with the children that he brought on a violent attack of asthma. . . he tumbled while skiing and strained his finger and last of all his shoulder was very stiff from carrying the skis." The thirty-eight-year-old father was still a model for the strenuous life!

In April 1897, President McKinley rewarded Roosevelt for his support by making him assistant secretary of the navy. McKinley admitted to one of Roosevelt's friends that he was a little worried about this nomination: "I am told that your friend Theodore is always getting into rows with everybody."

Roosevelt jumped into this position as quickly and completely as he had jumped into his other jobs. He was an expert on naval history, and his book *The Naval War of 1812* had convinced him of the importance of a strong navy. Edith, pregnant with their sixth child, would soon join him in Washington, glad to be back in the city she loved.

Secretary of the Navy John Long, a man who enjoyed vacations and long weekends, was content to let his new assistant take the lead. Less

---

Twelve-year-old Alice, photographed by her father.

than two months after he accepted the job, Roosevelt called for a bigger navy, more up-to-date ships, and better-trained seamen. The new assistant secretary cited possible threats from Japan and Spain in the Pacific and from Spain in the Caribbean. He declared that America was becoming a world power and needed a superior military force to protect that growth. "To be prepared for war is the most effectual means to promote peace."

With this declaration, Roosevelt made headlines all over the country. Most writers praised him for his vision of a strong America, but some suggested that he was too ready to go to war. He answered, "Better a thousand times err on the side of over-readiness to fight, than to err on the side of tame submission to injury, or cold-blooded indifference to the misery of the oppressed."

Roosevelt took advantage of Secretary Long's summer vacation in 1897 to advance naval preparedness. He opened a letter addressed to Long urging that Commodore John Howell be appointed commander-in-chief of the ships patrolling in the Pacific Ocean. This was the post that Roosevelt wanted for Commodore George Dewey, who shared his desire to increase American naval power in the Pacific. Roosevelt might have let the matter rest until Long's return, scheduled for the next day. Instead, he quickly persuaded a senator to press President McKinley to appoint Dewey. By the time Long arrived at the office, Dewey was the new commander-in-chief.

Roosevelt continued to work with almost superhuman speed. He inspected battleships, planned for press coverage of naval exercises, studied ways to improve storage of ships, investigated conditions in navy yards, drafted a personnel reform bill, and drew up an elaborate cruising schedule for the new torpedo-boat flotilla. "I'm having immense fun running the Navy," he reported.

Assistant Secretary of the Navy Roosevelt in his office.

Chapter 9
"Forward, March!"

Still, Roosevelt needed more challenge. He sold a collection of his essays and speeches, most of them focusing on the importance of individual and national patriotism, as a book called *American Ideals and other Essays Social and Political.* In October 1897, he campaigned for local Republican candidates in Massachusetts. He had written about half of the *The Winning of the West,* and he worked on outlines for the next four volumes. He also considered beginning a book about the Asian Mongol Tartars during the thirteenth and fourteenth centuries. He continued to work on publications with the B and C Club.

On November 19, Quentin, his sixth and last child, was born. Roosevelt was home when Edith went into labor. He reported, "With the aid of my bicycle I just got the Doctor and Nurse in time."

Roosevelt reacted sharply to reports that the Spanish government in Cuba was persecuting Americans and Cuban natives there. He announced that America must protect these innocent victims and should go to war against Spain. In a letter to a navy commander, he wrote that he would welcome war with Spain not only to stop the persecution but also because of "the benefit done to our people by giving them something to think about which isn't material gain, and especially the benefit

Colonel Roosevelt of the Rough Riders.

done to our military forces by trying both the Army and Navy in actual practice."

In a private letter, Roosevelt explained what he would do if he had the authority. As soon as the United States declared war against the Spanish in Cuba, he would send the Pacific fleet of the American navy to the Philippine Islands to take control from the Spanish there. These islands would become a strong Pacific naval base for America. Another part of his plan was that the United States would annex Hawaii to serve as a second Pacific naval base.

Some biographers wonder why Roosevelt was so quick to accept war as the answer to the Cuban problem. Some think that he was simply overreacting to the situation, perhaps to propel himself into the national limelight. Others suggest that because he had struggled so hard against illness as a child, he had developed an especially strong fighting instinct.

Certainly he had fed this instinct to fight while in the West where men lived by their physical strength and readiness to accept any challenge. As a result of that strenuous life, he had also developed self-confidence. He had learned to make quick decisions. In the West, a man was immediately judged either honest or crooked; there was often no time for negotiation or compromise.

Historians have noted that many leaders of Roosevelt's time were attracted to the challenge of combat. As Lord Wolseley, a British commander, wrote, "All other pleasures pale before the intense, the maddening delight of leading men into the midst of an enemy."

Some reporters in Cuba sent back exaggerated accounts: "American citizens are imprisoned or slain without cause. . . . Blood on the roadside, blood in the fields, blood on the doorsteps, blood, blood, blood!" These reporters were encouraged by their employers, William Randolph Hearst, owner of the *New York Journal*, and Joseph Pulitzer, owner of the New York *World*, who wanted to increase newspaper circulation. The newspaper stories attracted readers. They did not always portray a true picture of conditions.

Apparently Roosevelt believed these reports. He kept up pressure to build battleships and to train naval forces for combat. To those who said that the navy should be used only defensively, he said that attitude was "about as sensible as that of a prize fighter who expected to win by merely parrying instead of hitting." He begged Americans to help the Cubans who were subject to "murderous oppression."

In January 1898, President McKinley sent the battleship USS *Maine* to Havana Harbor in Cuba. The official message was that the ship came as "an act of friendly courtesy." Many observers saw an unofficial message. They believed the ship was a big stick, a warning to the Spanish of American readiness to protect Cuban and American citizens.

While docked in Havana Harbor on February 15, the *Maine* suddenly exploded and sank, killing more than two hundred fifty men.

The Senate asked for an investigation. American citizens coined a new slogan, "Remember the *Maine!*" Roosevelt demanded a declaration of war, saying, "The *Maine* was sunk by an act of dirty treachery on the part of the Spaniards, *I* believe."

Ten days later, with the investigation still in progress, Roosevelt was left in charge of the office for an afternoon. He sent a telegram to Commodore Dewey in the Philippines, ordering him to prepare for war against Spain. Dewey's assignment was to make sure that no Spanish ships left the Pacific to head for Cuba. Roosevelt sent similar orders to American commanders all over the world. He ordered huge supplies of ammunition for the navy and requested that Congress authorize recruitment of seamen.

The next day, when Long discovered what Roosevelt had done, he said that the assistant secretary had "come very near causing more of an explosion than happened to the *Maine*." He resolved never to leave

The New York World's *report of the* Maine *explosion.*

Roosevelt in charge again, but he did not change any of the orders.

Six weeks later, the Senate ended its investigation. The senators agreed that an explosion had caused the sinking, but they could not place the blame for the blast. (In 1976, the navy concluded that a fire on the *Maine* had ignited its ammunition and caused the ship to explode.)

President McKinley accepted the report. He had not wanted to believe that the Spanish had attacked an American ship. Now he was eager to forget the incident.

Roosevelt was furious. "McKinley has no more backbone than a chocolate eclair!" he exclaimed. He told Secretary Long that he was ready to lead a regiment to Cuba to show the Spanish that they could not get away with destroying a United States ship.

Political leaders and common citizens debated the situation. The slogan "Remember the *Maine!*" became more popular daily, and newspaper reports continued to inflame the country. At the end of April 1898, President McKinley yielded to public pressure. He asked Congress to vote on a motion to declare war against Spain. Congress voted in favor of the declaration.

Roosevelt immediately resigned from the navy so that he could fight in Cuba. Navy Secretary Long disagreed with this move. Long said, "He thinks he is following his highest ideal, whereas, in fact. . . he is acting like a fool."

Soon after the Spanish-American War was declared, Admiral Dewey's six ships destroyed the Spanish fleet in the Philippines. No Americans were lost. This victory brought new confidence in the American navy.

Secretary of War Russell Alger offered Roosevelt the command of the first regiment of volunteers to fight in Cuba. Citing his own inexperience, Roosevelt suggested that Leonard Wood, an admired friend, be given the command. Wood was named colonel, and Roosevelt lieutenant colonel.

The New York Times

ILLUSTRATED MAGAZINE SUPPLEMENT.

SIXTEEN PAGES. AUGUST 28, 1898. PRICE, FIVE CENTS.

On May 15, the new lieutenant colonel arrived in San Antonio, Texas, wearing a fawn-colored uniform with bright yellow trim, a uniform he had designed himself. He had had a dozen pairs of steel-rimmed spectacles sewn into his uniforms and equipment. Roosevelt wanted to be sure that he could see the enemy he had come to kill.

One thousand volunteers met him there, men who had answered his call for a regiment of patriots. He had worked with many of them in the past. They were an assortment of Western cowboys, athletes from Harvard and other colleges, business leaders, Native Americans, and gold prospectors. The press called this regiment "Roosevelt's Rough Riders" because, at first, they did not have the formal attitude and training expected of a troop of soldiers. Roosevelt assigned a rigorous program of mounted drill, skirmish practice, and dress parades. He wrote to his sister Corinne, "It is a great historical expedition, and I thrill to feel that I am part of it."

Other United States regiments also prepared for battle. In early June, six thousand Americans, including the Rough Riders, landed on the Cuban shore. Roosevelt was furious when he learned that Brigadier General William Shafter had refused to transport horses, except for the officers'.

The Rough Riders' first assignment was to march over seven miles of bug-infested road, the Camino Real, to a ridge called Kettle Hill. Just beyond that ridge was another hill, San Juan Hill. Here the Spanish controlled the all-important harbor at Santiago. The Americans planned to take San Juan Hill and to lay siege to Santiago.

Roosevelt rode up Kettle Hill at the head of his troops, a conspicuous target for the enemy. To the rim of his sombrero he had attached a blue polka-dot handkerchief, and this waved like a flag. To the foot soldiers who hung back, he shouted, "Are you afraid?"

At one point, he pushed forward so fast that he forgot to order his men

Colonel Roosevelt on horseback.

This painting shows the all-black Tenth Cavalry, which fought alongside the Rough Riders. Nearly one-quarter of the American soldiers in Cuba were black.

to follow. Of the five who did, two were killed while Roosevelt ran back and shouted at this regiment:

"What, are you cowards?"

"We are waiting for the command."

"Forward, march!"

Roosevelt's regiment lost seven times more men than any other volunteer regiment. Some historians have suggested that he sacrificed caution in his desire for victory. In 1902, Roosevelt spoke about the fact that death is a necessary part of war. As for attacking the enemy, he said that he was not "in the least sensitive about killing any number of men if there is adequate reason."

One historian, Edmund Morris, described the battle of Kettle Hill: "Suddenly so many thousands of bullets came down, ripping in sheets through grass and reeds and human bodies, that the mud of the crossing turned red, and the water flowing over it ran purple. . . . shrieking projectiles chugged into groins, hearts, lungs, limbs, and eyes."

In a letter to his sister Corinne, Roosevelt described the scene: "Flocks of vultures and buzzards, the dead and wounded lost in the tangled growth—and swarms of crabs—great big land crabs, with one, enormous, lobster-like claw, creeping, rustling, scuffling."

In spite of heavy losses, the Americans took Kettle Hill. From its crown, they fired at Spanish soldiers now visible in the San Juan Hill blockhouse.

Then Roosevelt gave the order to surge up San Juan Hill. Up raced the Rough Riders, through a stream, over a wire fence, zig-zagging around enemy bullets and shells. Now Santiago Harbor lay below them. The American infantry had joined the navy in a blockade of Santiago. The war would soon be over.

After a siege of less than three weeks, the Spanish in Santiago surrendered. On July 17, 1898, the Stars and Stripes were raised over the

Santiago fort. Roosevelt said of the conflict, "Should the worst come to the worst, I am quite content to go now and to leave my children at least an honorable name."

On August 12, Spain agreed to give up control in Cuba. It also transferred Puerto Rico and Guam to United States authority. This transfer gave the United States its first overseas territory, and was an important factor in the growth of the U.S. as a world power. Spain also agreed to allow the United States to occupy Manila in the Philippine Islands until a long-term plan could be arranged.

The War Department planned to leave the troops in Cuba for an undetermined period to ensure peace. But yellow fever was spreading through the camps, food and medical supplies were low, and morale was down. Breaking an unwritten rule that a military man should never question an order publicly, Roosevelt encouraged other officers to sign an open letter which he sent to American newspapers. This letter demanded the immediate withdrawal of American troops from Cuba, ending with, "As the army can be safely moved now, the persons responsible for preventing such a move will be responsible for the unnecessary loss of many thousands of lives." The letter appeared in newspapers throughout the country on August 5, 1898, but the secretary of war had already decided to bring the men home. On August 15, the regiments landed on Long Island.

As the soldiers marched down the gangplanks of the transport *Miami*, bands blared and hundreds cheered. Vigorous and triumphant, Roosevelt showed no sign that he had contracted a touch of Cuban fever which would later sap his strength. He strolled over to a group of reporters, eager to talk about the "bully time and bully fight" he had enjoyed in Cuba.

One reporter shouted, "Will you be our next governor?"

"None of that," he answered. "All I'll talk about is the regiment. It's

THE VICTORIOUS
ROUGH RIDERS

Roosevelt and his Rough Riders.

the finest regiment that ever was, and I'm proud to command it."

Because of the yellow fever, the regiment was quarantined in Long Island for a few weeks. Not wanting to wait that long to see her husband, Edith managed to volunteer as a hospital assistant there. She tended the sick and wounded until August 20, when Theodore was free to leave for Oyster Bay.

Sagamore Hill swarmed with reporters. Roosevelt saw that the public was ready to reward him for his bravery in Cuba. Republican leaders, sensing this also, talked to him about running for governor of New York State. Two important party leaders agreed to support him, and Roosevelt promised them secretly that he would run. He also ordered the manufacture of ten thousand "Our Teddy for Governor" buttons.

However, he teased the public by pretending he had not made up his mind. The longer he teased, the more people shouted for him to run. On September 17, when Roosevelt had party leaders and the public waiting with great anticipation for his decision, he announced that he would consent to be the Republican candidate for governor. Edith, who preferred that he settle down to a quiet life as a writer, accepted his decision gracefully.

By the time Republican leaders officially announced his nomination on October 3, Roosevelt had already begun writing a series of articles on his war experiences. These later became a book, *The Rough Riders*.

Once in the race, Roosevelt charged ahead with his campaign as enthusiastically as he had charged up Kettle Hill. Probably his most important advantage was his fame as a military hero. And he made the most of it. Six Rough Riders in full uniform accompanied him everywhere. He wore a wide-brimmed hat modeled on the one he had worn in Cuba. He ordered that a bugler play to get the attention of the crowd just before he was introduced.

Roosevelt made as many as fifteen speeches a day, traveling through the state in a two-car railway train hired especially for his campaign. He gave his audiences what they wanted to hear — talk of patriotism, nationalism, and his experiences in Cuba.

Then he found another issue to appeal to voters. Richard Croker, a Tammany Hall boss, had openly refused to endorse Supreme Court Justice Joseph Daly for reelection. Croker said Daly had failed to rehire a staff worker recommended by Tammany Hall. Roosevelt made the issue a public one, and he promised an end to such corruption if elected.

A reporter at Carthage, New York, heard Roosevelt speak. He wrote: "The man's presence was everything, it was electrical, magnetic. . . . I looked in the faces of hundreds and saw only pleasure and satisfaction." Roosevelt gained more support as the economy took an upturn. Industrial production rose, and unemployment fell. Farmers obtained higher prices for their crops.

When the ballots were counted on November 8, 1898, Roosevelt had won by almost eighteen thousand votes. "I was lucky," he wrote to a friend. "First to get into the war; and then to get out of it; then to get elected."

Chapter 10
Governor Roosevelt
and the Big Stick

Immediately, Roosevelt ran into conflict with Senator Thomas Platt, who was called Boss Platt because of his status in the Republican party. Platt expected Roosevelt to reward faithful party workers with state jobs.

Roosevelt and Boss Platt disagreed over the appointment of a commissioner to oversee insurance practices in the state. Boss Platt and most of the insurance companies wanted Roosevelt to reappoint Louis Payn. But Roosevelt's investigation found that Payn had borrowed half a million dollars from a bank whose director was also a director of an insurance company. Roosevelt accused Payn of using the influence of his office as insurance regulator to obtain the loan.

Roosevelt tried compromise. He told Platt that he could choose from among three other men for the position. Platt refused.

Next, Roosevelt offered a big stick ultimatum. If Platt did not select a commissioner from the list within three days, he would not be allowed any choice in the selection.

A tenement street in New York City (about 1900).

Platt offered his own threat. If Roosevelt did not appoint Payn in three days, he would never again receive Platt's support.

On the third day, Platt's aide, Benjamin Odell, asked to see Roosevelt. Some of their conversation has been recorded:

> Odell: You have made up your mind?
> Roosevelt: I have.
> Odell: You know it means your ruin.
> Roosevelt: Well, we will see about that.
> Odell: You understand the fight will begin tomorrow and will
>   be carried on to the bitter end.
> Roosevelt: Yes. Good night.
> Odell: Hold on! We accept!

Writing about this in his autobiography, Roosevelt said he "never saw a bluff carried more resolutely through to the final limit."

In January 1899, Governor Roosevelt attacked the state taxation system, declaring that it was "in utter confusion, full of injustices."

He pointed to the corporations which provided basic public services such as streetcars, gas and electric power, and water. He declared that these corporations should pay state taxes for the privilege, called a *franchise*, of using state land and resources to meet public needs. He argued that the franchises gave the corporations a monopoly on public services and thus guaranteed them a profit. A franchise tax bill would require that the corporations pay for the privilege of enjoying a monopoly.

Platt disagreed. He said that corporations should not be taxed for providing vital services. Corporation representatives warned Roosevelt that if he voted for the franchise tax bill, they would finance his opponents every time he ran for office.

Roosevelt would not budge. Speaking in the Senate, he said of the bill, "I cannot too strongly urge its immediate passage."

After he spoke, he worried. He confided to a fellow assemblyman, "I suppose I have ended my political career today."

The assemblyman answered, "You're mistaken, Governor. This is only the beginning."

Finally, legislators passed a bill which required tax payments from certain corporations. This quieted some of the reformers while it did not severely hurt the large corporations.

It was becoming clear, to Roosevelt and others, that the government would have to watch closely over the growing and changing nation. "Our attitude should be one of correcting the evils," he wrote.

New situations would require new approaches. Between 1860 and 1900, about fourteen million immigrants arrived in America, creating a rich and varied cultural mix. They also created a huge labor supply. Their need for immediate housing brought the growth of slums as landowners hastily erected tenements with little or no regard for sanitation, heat and light, and comfort. The rapidly expanding cities suffered from overcrowding, poverty, and lack of social planning. Immigrants also pushed onto the rich prairies of the West and into cities on the Pacific coast. Many performed backbreaking labor; others brought both money and ideas for economic growth.

Competition among industries grew. Some businesses merged to cut out competition. The mergers worked like this: two clothing manufacturers would agree to share such things as machinery, shipping facilities, buildings, and supplies. Their expenses decreased as a result of the sharing, and they lowered their prices. Customers flocked to them. Smaller clothing manufacturers could not compete, and they were forced out of business. Then, with no competition, the merged clothing manufacturers could raise prices back to the former levels, or to even higher ones.

The Sherman Antitrust Act of 1890 prohibited corporations from merging merely to cut out competition. But this act applied only to corporations doing interstate business (commerce in more than one state). Any business operating within the boundaries of a single state would be subject only to the regulations of that state.

Heads of interstate corporations insisted that mergers, which resulted in companies called *trusts*, were normal functions of businesses. They asserted that government had no right to interfere with these functions. Besides, they said, the trusts helped consumers by allowing businesses to offer lower prices.

In the early 1900s, over a million and a half children worked. In mines, they bent over for twelve hours a day, separating slate from coal in dark, chilly rooms. In factories, they ran heavy, dangerous machines. In cramped tenement apartments, they helped their parents make cigars and artificial flowers, and they carried loads of cloth upstairs and piles of finished clothing down for garment makers. Many children earned less than twenty-five cents a day. Of course, this money went into food, clothing, and shelter for the family. With this day's pay, the parents could buy a dozen eggs or several loaves of bread.

Adults were also overworked in unsafe and physically exhausting jobs. In 1900, seventy percent of American industrial laborers toiled ten or more hours each workday. Often, management was free to cut wages at any time, for immigration and the increasing population created an oversupply of labor.

There were some laws regulating job conditions. However, many workers were afraid to complain, fearing they might lose their jobs.

Labor unions tried to protect workers who protested against working conditions. But even the largest union, the American Federation of Labor, with one million members, offered little challenge to hostile employers, strikebreakers, and restrictions against unions.

Some workers appealed to the courts. Women pleaded for enforcement of a law forbidding employers to make them work at night. The

This photograph by Lewis Hine shows a girl working in a textile mill.

New York Court of Appeals declared that law unconstitutional since it would deny some women the right to work any time of day they wanted to. In 1905, the U.S. Supreme Court overthrew a law stating bakery workers did not have to work more than sixty hours a week. The court ruled that laws could not restrict the right of employers and employees to make their own work contracts. When injured workers or the families of workers injured on their jobs applied for workmen's compensation, they were turned down on the grounds that the worker could have refused the job.

Among those citizens who saw no need to enforce present laws or impose new ones was a small group of wealthy people who owned mansions, yachts, and private railroad cars. Many of them believed, as businessman John Rockefeller did, that "God gave me my money." They felt no concern for those to whom God did not give money.

Most federal and state officials believed that business and labor should work out their own solutions. They pointed to the fact that our country had prospered under policies that encouraged initiative and competition. They were reluctant to restrict these basic principles of capitalism.

Roosevelt also believed that free competition was healthy. However, his experience as a political leader led him to develop his idea of a *square deal*—an equal opportunity for everyone—and to consider government interference where necessary to ensure this.

In 1892 and 1894, two especially large and violent strikes occurred. In the summer of 1892, wage negotiations between management and a union broke down at the Carnegie Steel Company in Homestead, Pennsylvania. Henry Clay Frick, chairman of the board, did not follow the customary procedure of shutting down the mills until a settlement could be reached. Instead, he brought in strikebreakers to continue the work.

When the strikers fought against the men sent to replace them, Frick sent in three hundred private detectives. They were attacked by the

This drawing of the Homestead strike shows the strikers in control as the detectives leave barges they had arrived in.

workers, who had many weapons including dynamite and a small cannon. After a thirteen-hour fight in which seven people were killed, the strikers seemed to be in control for a few days. Then, at Frick's request, the Pennsylvania governor sent in eight thousand militiamen. The soldiers defeated the strikers. Company officials took back a few workers and hired many new ones. Four months after negotiations failed, the company was back in full operation, and the union was destroyed.

In May 1894, workers for the Pullman railway sleeping car company voted to strike after their wages were cut by about one-third. Some railway workers struck in sympathy. Declaring that a continuing strike would create a national emergency, President Cleveland sent in soldiers. Strikers went back to work only after their leader was jailed and twenty-five workers killed. This was the first important case in which a president used the federal government to break a strike.

In Buffalo in May 1899, the American Federation of Labor supported two thousand dockside workers who refused to shovel grain from the ships. The workers objected that their wages were cut when management changed the payment from $1.85 for every one thousand bushels unloaded to twenty-five cents an hour.

Governor Roosevelt sent in a mediator, a person who helps to settle disputes. At the same time, he advised the state militia to be ready to send men to Buffalo. Although several fights took place between workers and management, Roosevelt's big stick, the threat of military intervention, probably prevented widespread disturbances. In two weeks, the protest was over. Each side declared at least partial victory, and Roosevelt took credit for solving a major dispute.

Early in April 1900, seven hundred fifty laborers seized a half-finished dam in Westchester County, New York. They threatened to keep control until their wages were raised. The employers hired one hundred armed deputies to take back the dam.

This time, Roosevelt did not merely threaten with his big stick; he sent two companies of militia to the scene. He also ordered a mediator to work with both sides. As the strike wore on, immigrants were hired to take the places of the striking workers. By late April, a full work force was in place, and workers who were still on strike lost their jobs.

Roosevelt was not satisfied with the results of these work stoppages. He admitted, "We are powerless to make the contractors give larger wages, though I myself personally think the wages are too low."

Although he met with union officials more than any New York governor before him, Roosevelt maintained his belief that business, not government, should set the standards for working conditions. Further, he believed that the problems resulted not from too few laws, but from "the lack of proper means to enforce existing laws." He believed that government officials had both the right and the responsibility to interfere in certain situations. He had done this himself by insisting on mediation in strikes while sending troops to keep control.

Roosevelt was also troubled about living conditions in the tenements. In his second term in the Assembly, he had seen the cigarmakers' apartments with Samuel Gompers. As police commissioner, he had walked the streets of New York's poor neighborhoods. He knew that many apartments were firetraps with unsanitary plumbing, shoddy construction, poor heating, and unspeakable filth. He described them: "The tenement house in its worst shape is a festering sore. . . . We cannot be excused if we fail to cut out this ulcer." He pushed for enforced regulation of sanitary and safety conditions.

Roosevelt also supported bills for shorter workdays for women and children and state safety inspection of factories. When these bills passed, he appointed inspectors to oversee enforcement of the new rules. He was applauded by working people, social workers, union officials, and citizens who believed that reform was needed. He was criticized by businessmen, financiers, and conservative politicians who believed that government had no right to interfere with business.

William McKinley, president from 1897 to 1901.

As cities grew and spread into the countryside, Roosevelt feared the destruction of the clean waters, forests, and open spaces he loved so much. He investigated the New York State Fisheries, Forest, and Game Commission, and what he found enraged him. The commission was not monitoring the use of timber resources. Lumbermen were cutting trees with no concern for soil erosion, and they were not planting new ones.

Governor Roosevelt insisted that the state develop a scientific forestry policy with cutting guidelines to foster growth of new trees, tree-planting experiments, and studies of the use of trees to prevent erosion. He received help from Gifford Pinchot, chief forester of the United States. He appointed a commission to establish public parks. He also transferred responsibility for New York City's water supply from a private business to city government.

Investigations! Changes! Reform! Regulations! Many New York politicians thought Roosevelt had gone too far. When President William

McKinley needed a vice-presidential candidate in 1900, these leaders nominated Roosevelt in order to remove him from New York State politics.

Roosevelt was not eager to become vice-president. He said he believed that he could accomplish more as governor, and that as vice-president he would merely be an echo of the president. Besides, he was not the kind of man to work in the shadow of another.

Edith did not want him to become vice-president, either. She liked living in the governor's home in Albany. And Theodore made ten thousand dollars a year as governor; as vice-president, he would make only eight thousand.

But all over the country, citizens saw him as a hero: he hunted big game, had proved his courage in Cuba, and spoke out against wrongdoing and injustice.

One group of admirers was a Kansas delegation to the Republican national convention in June 1900. They barged in on Roosevelt in his hotel room without even knocking. They marched around him playing fifes, drums, and bugles and chanting, "We want Teddy! We want Teddy!" He protested that he wanted to remain a governor, but the delegates paid no attention. They marched and chanted some more. Then they marched out.

Other delegations from other states also dramatized their support for Roosevelt. He was so well known that he received a letter from Arizona with no address. Drawn on the envelope were a set of large teeth and a pair of spectacles!

On June 21, Edith watched the proceedings from a gallery box at the convention. Wearing a black hat and skirt and a pink blouse, she attracted the attention of reporters who declared that she was interesting, if not beautiful. As Theodore rose to the podium to second McKinley's nomination, he waved at her. She smiled back.

Vice-presidential candidate Roosevelt at an outdoor rally in New York State.

She continued to smile as Theodore accepted the nomination for vice-president. Edith would not be a drawback to Theodore's career.

The new candidate pledged to campaign for McKinley against his opponent, William Jennings Bryan. "I am as strong as a bull moose," he said, "and you can use me to the limit." In the next four months, three million Americans became acquainted with his toothy grin and with the spectacles that always seemed about to fly off his face. They were fascinated by his high, squeaky voice and the way he smashed his fist onto his palm to emphasize points as he talked.

He campaigned from the first light of day, as milk wagons began to make their rounds, until late in the evening. He spoke from the backs of trains all across the West and from the podium in Madison Square Garden in New York City. He traveled over three thousand miles in thirty-two days, making an average of nine speeches a day. One of his friends said he talked "like a repeating rifle, spat, spat, spat."

In agreement with the Republican party platform, Roosevelt urged that the United States continue to back its paper money with gold, not silver, as Bryan had proposed. Republicans believed that this "gold standard" would keep the country's economy stable. Roosevelt also spoke in favor of protective tariffs to increase the price of imported goods, giving American manufacturers an advantage. He believed that federal government regulations should override state and local regulations when there was a conflict. The candidate often repeated the favorite Republican slogan, "A full dinner pail for all." At one point, his train was slowing down for a bridge as it entered North Dakota. A woman rushed up to give him some live chickens. He held them high and shouted, "Look, a full dinner pail!"

On November 6, 1900, the Republicans won a sweeping victory, and Roosevelt became vice-president-elect. He was inaugurated on March 4, 1901, and he presided over the Senate for just five days until March 9, when it closed. His official duties would begin again in December, when the Senate would next meet. Until then, Roosevelt planned to write and to spend time with his family. He also took up the study of law that he had dropped thirteen years ago, intending to become a lawyer after his term as vice-president.

His vacation lasted just six months. An assassin killed McKinley. On September 14, 1901, the forty-two-year-old Roosevelt was sworn in as the twenty-sixth president of the United States. He was the youngest man ever to become president.

The Roosevelt family in 1903. From left: Quentin,
Theodore, Ted, Archie, Alice, Kermit, Edith, and Ethel.

Chapter 11

Trusts, Strikes, and Panama

Although the new president promised the grieving nation that he would move slowly and follow McKinley's footsteps, many citizens were not reassured. Roosevelt was not only the youngest president; he was, in many ways, the most unusual. Senator Marcus Hanna of Ohio had openly called him "that damn cowboy." Yet, as others noted, he was interested in literature and the songs of birds. He even wrote books! He had risen to the highest political office with amazing speed. He had confronted both government officials and party leaders as assemblyman, Civil Service commissioner, police chief, and governor. As assistant secretary of the Navy, he had issued critical orders to the fleet without the consent of his superior. He had left that post abruptly to lead a group of cowboys, college graduates, and businessmen to battle. What might this unpredictable man do now that he held the big stick of the presidency?

Even the president's family was surprising. When they moved into the White House, they brought an assortment of dogs, cats, guinea pigs, snakes, and lizards!

In his first annual message to Congress, in December 1901, Roosevelt

praised the "captains of industry," saying they "have on the whole done great good to our people." However, he added, legislation was required to counteract the "real and grave evils" of large industry as the economy grew and as interstate commerce increased.

The business world was shocked two months later when Roosevelt asked his attorney general, Philander Knox, to invoke the Sherman Antitrust Act against a company recently created by J. P. Morgan. The company, the Northern Securities Company, was a merger of railroads. It now controlled shipping throughout most of the West. Morgan and other officers in the trust also had interests in many other companies which produced goods. With their extended control of the railroads, they could raise the shipping rates of their various manufacturing competitors and drive them out of business.

Company officials protested Roosevelt's move. They complained that the president himself had admitted that the Sherman Act was somewhat vague. Besides, they said, Roosevelt should have warned them before he took action. J. P. Morgan said to Roosevelt, "If we have done anything wrong, send your man [the attorney general] to my man [one of Morgan's lawyers] and they can fix it up."

Roosevelt answered, "That can't be done."

Until this time, the Sherman Act had not interfered seriously with any large corporations. However, now companies feared the legislation. All over the country, businessmen warned that Roosevelt was going to destroy the American economy. One newspaper reported: "Not since the assassination of President McKinley has the stock market had such a sudden shock."

Not everybody opposed the president's action. One paper said sarcastically, "Wall Street is paralyzed at the thought that a President of the United States should sink so low as to try to enforce the law."

Lawyers debated the case until March 1904, when the Supreme

Roosevelt gives a speech in Asheville, North Carolina (1902).

Court agreed with Roosevelt. The Northern Securities Company was divided into smaller companies. During Roosevelt's presidency, forty-three other large companies were sued under the Sherman Act. Roosevelt became known as a "trust buster." Some considered this a compliment; others said it scornfully. However, regulation rather than destruction of trusts remained his aim.

Another kind of problem arose when the new president invited Dr. Booker T. Washington, a prominent black educator, to the White House. Some citizens were incensed. The *New Orleans Times Democrat* said, "White men of the South, how do you like it? When Mr. Roosevelt sits down to dinner with a Negro, he declares that the Negro is the social equal of the white man." Roosevelt answered that he would dine with anyone he pleased. But he never again invited a black citizen to the White House.

In 1902, the teddy bear was "invented." On a bear hunt in Mississippi, men in Roosevelt's hunting party chased a cub until it was exhausted. Then they tied it to a tree so that Roosevelt could kill it. Roosevelt refused to take advantage of the situation and shoot the tortured bear for sport. Clifford Berryman, a cartoonist for the Washington *Post*, drew a cartoon of Roosevelt refusing to shoot the bear. The story was picked up by reporters, and in no time, toymakers were marketing "teddy bears."

In the same year, Roosevelt met one of his most difficult labor-management conflicts. In May 1902, Pennsylvania coal workers went on strike. They demanded higher wages, shorter hours, and safer working conditions. They also demanded the right to live and shop where they pleased, instead of being forced to rent company-owned homes and to shop in company-owned stores.

Irving Stone, a novelist, later wrote about the mines: "Six men out of a thousand were killed every year; hundreds were maimed by explosions and cave-ins; few escaped the ravages of asthma, bronchitis, chronic

This famous cartoon shows Roosevelt refusing to kill the bear.

This cartoon shows the president proclaiming the square deal. The caption reads, "Laying the Foundations."

rheumatism, consumption, heart trouble. By the age of fifty the miners were worn out and broken."

One typical mine operator, George Baer, refused to talk with the workers, saying, "The rights and interests of the laboring man will be protected and cared for . . . by the Christian men to whom God in His infinite wisdom has given control of the property interests of the country."

Roosevelt created a commission to study working conditions in mines. He asked both labor and management to accept whatever the commission recommended. The workers agreed. The mine operators did not. Roosevelt said afterward of Baer, "If it wasn't for the high office I hold, I would have taken him by the seat of the breeches and the nape of the neck and chucked him out that window."

Autumn was approaching, and homes, factories, stores, schools, and hospitals would soon need heat supplied by coal. Roosevelt pulled out his big stick. If management refused to cooperate, he would ask the governor of Pennsylvania to request federal troops to seize the mines. The troops would operate the mines until the conflict was settled.

The operators gave in. In March 1903, the commission recommended higher pay and shorter working hours for the miners. It did not, however, grant recognition to their union. The commission also recommended that the operators be allowed to raise the price of coal by ten percent to take care of their new higher costs. Both sides accepted these recommendations.

Roosevelt was a hero. He had ended the strike. Both workers and management had won in what he called a square deal. The government had played an important role by ensuring that both sides were treated impartially.

Roosevelt wrote in his autobiography: "The old familiar intimate relations between employer and employee were passing. A few generations before, the boss had known every man in his shop. . . he swapped jokes and stories and perhaps a bit of tobacco with them. There was no such relation between [the men] who controlled the anthracite industry, and the one hundred and fifty thousand men who worked in the mines, or the half million women and children who were dependent on these miners for their daily bread."

As the population grew, bosses could always find other employees, but employees could not as easily find other jobs. Workers tried to form unions to negotiate job protection for themselves. Management fought against unions.

The president understood why some citizens were opposed to unions. He wrote in his autobiography: "They note the unworthy conduct of many labor leaders, they find instances of bad work by union men, of a voluntary restriction of output, of vexatious and violent strikes." On the other hand, the president added, "If I were a factory employee, a workman on the railroads or a wage-earner of any sort, I would undoubtedly join the union of my trade. If I disapproved of its policy, I would join in order to fight that policy; if the union leaders were dishonest, I would join in order to put them out."

Many members of the conservative Congress disagreed with the president's views. Their strong business ties led them to oppose Roosevelt's interpretation of a square deal.

In December 1902, Roosevelt turned his attention south. Germany and Great Britain were attempting to collect money owed them by Venezuela, a country in South America. They seized several Venezuelan ships, and blockaded the coast. Then German ships fired on two forts.

This might seem to be of little interest to Theodore Roosevelt and other United States leaders since Venezuela was far away. But President Roosevelt saw the incident as a violation of the Monroe Doctrine of 1823. This doctrine, formulated by President James Monroe and his

Cabinet, declared the United States would forbid any extension of European power in the Western Hemisphere (North and South America).

The British and Germans answered that they were merely collecting what was owed them, not extending their power. Roosevelt then took out his big stick; he ordered the United States battle fleet to Trinidad, seven miles off the coast of Venezuela.

The British and the Germans agreed to negotiate with Venezuela with Roosevelt as the mediator. The president convinced both sides to settle the conflict peacefully. For this work, he gained an international reputation as a negotiator.

In his December 1904 message to Congress, the president declared that the United States could intervene in the affairs of other Western Hemisphere countries to prevent Europeans from becoming involved. This declaration was called the Roosevelt Corollary to the Monroe Doctrine, and it angered many Latin Americans.

Roosevelt believed in a strong and ready navy. The United States' problem lay in the wide expanse of land between the Atlantic and Pacific oceans. The only way for the fleet on one coast to come to the aid of the fleet on the other was by a long journey around the tip of South America. During the Spanish-American War, the USS *Oregon*, a part of the Pacific fleet, had to travel this route to join the U.S. forces in Cuba.

President Roosevelt had started to work on this problem earlier. In June 1902, he had received congressional permission to negotiate with Colombian leaders to build a canal in that part of their country called Panama. At its narrowest point, this strip of land, which separates the Pacific Ocean from the Caribbean Sea, was only thirty-one miles wide. A canal there would allow ships to pass quickly from the Atlantic to the Pacific. The Colombian leaders agreed. However, when the Americans offered ten million dollars in gold and an annual rent of two hundred fifty thousand dollars, the Colombians demanded more money.

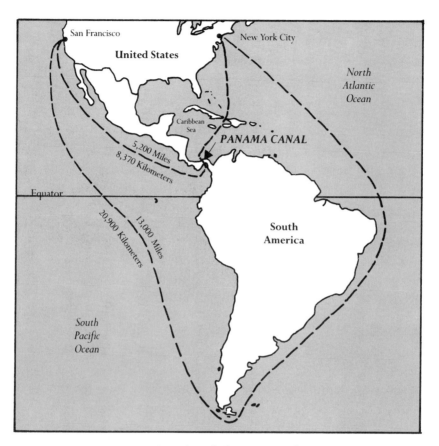

The Panama Canal and the surrounding area.

"Blackmail!" shouted Roosevelt to some of his friends. "Privately, I freely say to you that I should be delighted if Panama were an independent State."

In November 1903, the Panamanians did break away from Colombia. President Roosevelt rushed United States ships to the aid of the rebels. With U.S. help, the rebels won independence.

Many citizens, both American and Colombian, believed that the Panamanian revolt was not mere coincidence. They recalled how eager Roosevelt had been to use American troops in Cuba in 1898. Even members of Roosevelt's own Cabinet suspected that he had incited the revolt by secretly promising United States protection and support to the Panamanians.

Roosevelt denied the accusations. However, six years later, without discussing how he had achieved it, he said, "I took the Canal Zone."

In return for American assistance in the revolution, the new leaders of Panama gave the United States the right to build a canal there.

Chapter 12

A Strenuous Presidency

Roosevelt ran for the presidency against Democrat Alton Parker in 1904. As he campaigned for his first full term in office, Roosevelt boasted of his achievements. He had cleared the way to build the Panama Canal; prosecuted many antitrust suits; mediated the German/British/Venezuelan conflict; and negotiated the end of the Pennsylvania coal strike. He had demonstrated his belief in a square deal for both business and labor.

He had tried to please both sides on the controversial issue of tariffs on imported goods. Democrats generally favored reduced tariffs because they led to lower prices on the goods. Republicans generally opposed a reduction: they did not want imported goods to cost less than American-made ones. Roosevelt declared that the tariff issue should be studied, but he did not announce definite plans for this study.

Because of his trust-busting and his sympathy with working people, Roosevelt did not have the support of all Republicans. One corporation leader started a Stop Roosevelt movement which spread to New Jersey and some Southern states. The head of a railway system started the same movement in the West. Several anti-Roosevelt slogans focused on the need for a "safe and sane" president.

This famous cartoon by Davenport helped to get Roosevelt elected in 1904. In it, Uncle Sam says, "He's good enough for me."

Roosevelt at the polling place at Oyster Bay.

These opponents worked in vain. When the electoral vote was counted, Roosevelt had won by 336 to 140. He declared, "I am stunned by the overwhelming victory we have won." Then he added, "Under no circumstances will I be a candidate for or accept another nomination." Edith Roosevelt was as shocked as everyone else to hear that.

Roosevelt took office with one of the grandest inauguration parades in the history of the country. Crowds cheered as West Point officers and naval cadets in full uniform, governors on horseback, cowboys waving lassos, Native Americans in full dress, and one hundred fifty Harvard men in black caps and gowns marched around Washington for hours.

The White House police with some members of the White House gang.

The president thoroughly enjoyed his life in the White House. At the time of the second inauguration, the Roosevelt children ranged in age from Alice, who was twenty-one, to Quentin, who was eight. They were well known to the public as the "White House gang." All America laughed at stories of their bringing pets—including a pony and some snakes—into the presidential mansion. One story tells how Roosevelt had to scold his sons for throwing spitballs at an elegant portrait of President Andrew Jackson. The Roosevelt children roller skated and bicycled on the White House hardwood floors. They clumped up and down the stairs on stilts.

The North Room at Sagamore Hill. The head of an
American buffalo is on the wall.

Roosevelt had one set of goals for his girls and one set for his boys. He wanted both daughters to be "wise, with a well-trained mind, thoroughly awake to all that is going on in the world." He wanted each of his sons to "use his fighting instincts on the side of righteousness." Speaking to his children, he often sounded like a coach: "Don't flinch, don't foul, hit the line hard." His devotion to the strenuous life was evident to all who worked for and with him.

His own exercise plan included boxing with an army officer. Unfortunately, one day the officer hit him in the left eye with such force that small blood vessels were smashed, leaving him with limited sight. Roosevelt decided that he was too old to box, so he took up jujitsu, a form of self-defense.

At Sagamore Hill, he often played with his own children and those of relatives. He led them on what he called "obstacle walks." The children

The White House dining room during Roosevelt's presidency.
Mixed with the formal furnishings are animal heads.

had to do exactly what he did—whether it was pushing through briars, wading through a pond, or climbing over haystacks. The rule was to always go "over and through," never around an obstacle. This is the way he said he wanted to live his life, cutting straight through problems, never avoiding them.

Roosevelt played tennis on the White House lawn with a group of friends and advisors so often that the players became known as the Tennis Cabinet. They played in blazing heat, pouring rain, and snowstorms. The men also enjoyed boxing, wrestling, tossing medicine balls, hiking on steep rocks, and drinking mint juleps on the lawn.

On some winter days, spectators gathered to see their president swim through floating chunks of ice on the Potomac River.

Edith spent hours with designers, painters, and carpenters, creating more comfortable living quarters for her family and more gracious accommodations for White House guests. In an area once filled with boilers and pipes, she created an impressive gallery of portraits and busts of First Ladies. This display is still a popular White House attraction.

President Roosevelt faced many problems as he began his second term. Early in 1905, work began on the Panama Canal, and a yellow-fever epidemic struck the workers there. This was not a complete surprise; earlier, French attempts to build a canal had been doomed by malaria and yellow fever.

Workers deserted by the hundreds. When one ship arrived in July 1905 with new workers, more men were waiting on the dock to sail back home than were on the ship.

The seven-man Canal Commission believed that cleanliness and fresh paint would drive out the disease. Dr. William Gorgas, whom Roosevelt appointed chief sanitation engineer, disagreed. He had conquered yellow fever in Cuba three years before, and he knew that the disease was transmitted to humans by the bite of an infected mosquito.

Roosevelt agreed with Gorgas, not with the commission. He ordered that Gorgas be given the men and materials he asked for.

Under Gorgas' direction, all houses in the Canal Zone were fumigated, one hundred ten trillion square yards of swamp were drained and filled in, and marshes and swamps were oiled to kill mosquito larvae. Two hundred tons of wire-and-copper mesh were used to make screens for every house in the Canal Zone. Six months after this work was completed, yellow fever was almost completely wiped out.

Soon malaria, a serious disease spread by another mosquito, was also conquered.

As work on the canal proceeded, Roosevelt was involved in another situation beyond America's borders. In 1904, the Japanese had attacked the Russian fleet, and the Russo-Japanese War erupted. In 1905, the

Roosevelt sits in a steam shovel during digging at the canal site.

The president with Russian and Japanese representatives during the Russo-Japanese War settlement.

president offered to help the two countries reach a peaceful settlement. Although each side was reluctant, neither rejected the offer. Roosevelt's task was not easy. He wrote that he tried "to be polite and sympathetic and patient while explaining for the hundredth time something perfectly obvious, when what I really want is to give utterance to whoops of rage and jump up and knock their heads together."

Finally, Roosevelt convinced the representatives to sign a peace treaty at Portsmouth, New Hampshire, in August 1905. That treaty added to his reputation as an international peacemaker. In 1906, he was awarded the Nobel Peace Prize for his efforts. He was the first American to win that prize. He and Edith agreed that the best use of the forty-thousand-dollar prize money would be to establish an international committee to study improvement of relations between workers and management.

Some Americans objected that Roosevelt involved the United States in other countries' business. They preferred to isolate, or separate, America from the rest of the world. These *isolationists* objected again in early 1906 when Roosevelt called for a conference of European nations. The purpose was to discuss a threat of war from the German ruler, Wilhelm II.

The conference was a success, and again, the president was hailed as a peacemaker.

Early in his second term, Roosevelt asked citizens to help conserve the country's natural resources. Conservation was a new idea to most Americans, who believed that their nation had endless open space, clean air and water, and valuable forests. Until Roosevelt exposed the facts, Americans were unaware that more than half of the country's pine, fir, spruce, and redwood trees had been cut by loggers and miners. The cutting had left vast amounts of topsoil with no protection from wind and water erosion. And citizens did not realize that industrialization and the

Westward movement had brought air and water pollution just as surely as they had brought economic development.

President Roosevelt warned that careless use of forests threatened the extinction of buffalo, elk, and other animals. He criticized operators of coal and iron ore mines who caused destruction of land and waste of minerals.

The president was knowledgeable about conservation, and he was dedicated to it. As governor of New York, he had worked with conservationist Gifford Pinchot to establish a state forestry policy. As president, he created the United States Forest Service in 1905 with Pinchot as the head. Responsibilities of the service included reclaiming dry lands through irrigation, setting aside national forests, and creating wildlife refuges.

Roosevelt was also concerned about the practices of railroads, the main transporters of goods. Increasingly, shippers complained about railroad policies and prices. In 1903, Congress had passed the Elkins Act. It prohibited rebates, a kind of bonus awarded to companies which used the railroads most frequently. Rebates lowered transportation costs, allowing businesses to lower prices. This effectively cut smaller companies out of the competition. Owners of small businesses claimed that rates should be the same for all customers since federal and state money had helped to build the rail system.

Roosevelt used the term *malefactors*, meaning criminals, to describe businessmen who schemed against free competition. He insisted that each businessman had a right to a square deal, "as nearly as may be a fair chance to do what his powers permit him to do." He worked successfully for passage of the Hepburn Bill of 1906, which gave the Interstate Commerce Commission the right to determine the highest rates that railroads could charge.

Rapid growth of the population and economy had created another

---

Roosevelt and naturalist John Muir at Yosemite (1903).

serious problem: corruption that resulted in dreadful living and working conditions. In the early 1900s, a flow of books and articles exposed dishonest practices in such places as the Standard Oil Company, the meatpacking industry, city governments, and even the United States Senate. Many of these reports were factual; others were wild and sensational.

Popular magazines printed the reports; readers eagerly read and discussed them. All over the country, citizens asked: how can our government allow such practices?

Roosevelt admitted that some of the journalists served the country well with their reports. However, he criticized those who exaggerated the problems simply to attract readers. He called these sensationalists *muckrakers*—people who revealed weaknesses and evils with little concern about improving conditions. But in 1906, one book of fiction by a so-called muckraker changed the lives of working people in America forever. In *The Jungle*, Upton Sinclair pictured the filth of the meatpacking houses and the wretched lives of the workers. Some of his characters worked in the killing yards. They described their jobs: "You were apt to be covered with blood, and it would freeze solid. The men would tie up their feet in newspapers and old sacks, and these would be soaked in blood and frozen again. . . . When the bosses were not looking you would see them plunge their feet and ankles into the steaming hot carcass of the steer."

No inspectors came to the cutting yards or to the kitchens where sausages were made from ingredients like moldy older sausages, meat that had fallen in the dirt and sawdust of the floor, and meat that had been stored in huge piles in rooms where rats ran wild. No examiners supervised the annual cleaning of the waste barrels: "In the barrels would be dirt and rust and old nails and stale water—and cartload after cartload of it would be taken out and dumped into the hoppers with fresh meat, and sent out to the public's breakfast."

Roosevelt speaking from a train (1902 or 1906).

Sinclair wrote to Roosevelt demanding action against the meat packers. Roosevelt ordered an investigation of the situation. He told Sinclair that "the specific evils you point out shall, if their existence be proved, and if I have power, be eradicated."

The investigation turned up what Roosevelt labeled a "sickening report" on conditions in the industry. Managers of meat-packing houses denied the report. Thomas Wilson of the Nelson Morris Company was a typical packing industry boss. He insisted that his plant was "as clean as any kitchen."

Since the meat packers refused to supervise themselves, Roosevelt insisted on government monitoring. As he worked with Congress to develop regulations, Roosevelt showed his big stick to the meat packers: if they lobbied against the proposed legislation, he would expose more horror stories.

Both lobbyists and meat packers feared publicity. In June 1906, the Pure Food and Drug Act and the Meat Inspection Act were passed, prohibiting the sale of unclean food and medicine in interstate commerce. These laws did not eliminate all risks to public health, but they were a big step forward. Theodore Roosevelt had helped to get a square deal for the American consumer.

Roosevelt in his study at Sagamore Hill (1905).

Chapter 13
Troubles and Triumphs

In February 1906, the Roosevelt family made social news when twenty-two-year-old Alice married Nicholas Longworth, a Republican congressman, at the White House.

Roosevelt made news of another kind a few months later. In June, he agreed with the Spelling Reform Association that the spelling of three hundred common words should be simplified. Changes included: mamma to mama, waggon to wagon, hiccough to hiccup, though to tho, wished to wisht, honour to honor, dropped to dropt. Some citizens laughed, and some scoffed; few accepted the idea. Four months later, Roosevelt gave up on the reform publicly. But he did not give up privately. "In my own correspondence," he told the leader of the association, "I shall continue to use the new spelling."

In August of that same year, Roosevelt took charge in a black-white conflict. A group of black soldiers stationed in Brownsville, Texas, allegedly killed a white bartender and wounded a policeman in a rampage through the town. The townspeople, mostly white, were eager to convict the accused soldiers.

Since no eyewitness could identify the guilty soldiers, Roosevelt

A cartoonist pokes fun at Roosevelt's simplified spelling.

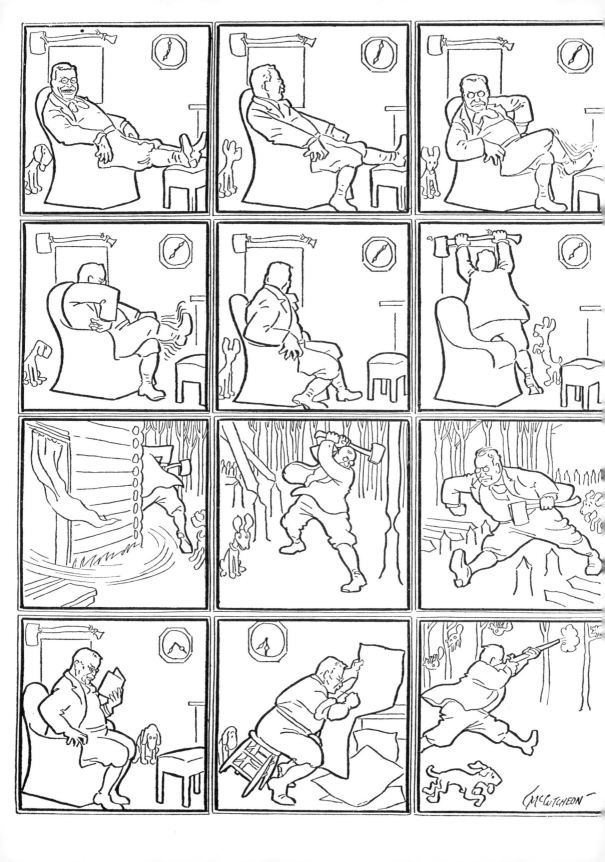

asked those who were innocent to name those who were guilty. No one responded. In November, he ordered that all one hundred sixty men of the black companies be dishonorably discharged, without a trial.

Many Southerners agreed that the discharge was justified. Many Northerners were outraged to learn that the accused soldiers were not granted their constitutional right to a trial before they were punished. Most blacks condemned the act. Booker T. Washington tried to blunt the criticism by reminding fellow blacks that Roosevelt "has favored them [blacks] in nine cases out of ten and the intelligent portion of the race does not believe that it is fair or wise to condemn such good friends as President Roosevelt."

Roosevelt supported blacks in other ways, however. He announced that he intended to appoint a black to a high federal post in Ohio. In his annual message to Congress in 1906, he spoke against lynching (killings by mobs, often committed against blacks), and he appealed for better education for blacks. He also told the army to consider organizing a black battalion of heavy artillery. In 1908, he served notice that a railway company must provide facilities for black passengers.

In the Brownsville incident, Roosevelt had echoed the superior attitude of many white citizens. American-born white males, who possessed most of the power in the United States at that time, also imposed this attitude of superiority on immigrants and women.

About immigrants, Roosevelt wrote: "The masses of foreigners will take at least a couple of generations before they can be educated to the proper point."

He explained his position on women to Susan B. Anthony: "I have always favored allowing women to vote, but I will say frankly that I do not attach the importance to it that you do." Earlier, he had written in his Harvard thesis that women should be allowed to vote. However, he had noted that men's commitment to voting was stronger than women's

This cartoon (about 1906) shows the energetic president "resting" while on vacation.

because "the men can fight in defense of their rights."

In 1907, Roosevelt's dedication to conservation was tested once again. Potential investors in rich mining, lumber, and grazing lands convinced their legislators to write an amendment to an agricultural bill. Under this amendment, the president would no longer have the power to create or expand forest reserves in Oregon, Washington, Idaho, Montana, Colorado, or Wyoming. That power would be transferred to the Congress, which was more easily controlled by outside influences.

The president had just eight days to respond to the agricultural bill, which he approved of, and the amendment, which he did not. He worked with men from the Forest Service around the clock to create twenty-one new reserves in the states listed. At one point, the men ran out of paper. Instead of waiting for a fresh supply, they continued drawing their forest-reserve maps on the floor. Roosevelt signed the measure, including the amendment, but before he did, he had added sixteen million acres to forest reserves, forever free from commercial use.

In 1905 and 1906, business prospered in the United States. Investors eagerly borrowed money to finance new projects, and customers eagerly bought their products and services. In 1907, the demand for new products slowed down. Investors were left with debts they could not repay. Because banking practices were not regulated, many banks had lent money without sufficient funds to back the loans. When businesses failed, so did the banks. All this led to unemployment for workers and panic among investors and other citizens.

In November 1907, Judge Elbert Gary, president of the United States Steel Corporation, suggested to President Roosevelt that the national economy would fall to a new low if a large company, the Tennessee Coal and Iron Company, were allowed to fail. Speaking for U.S. Steel, Gary offered to buy the company. United States Steel would incorporate the smaller company into its holdings and invest in it so that it would become again a source of both jobs and products. In return, Gary asked for a guarantee against prosecution under the Sherman Antitrust Act.

Overruling some of his advisers, the president agreed to the plan. The agreement was an example of his square deal philosophy, for it would help both business and workers. Some historians think Roosevelt was so eager to settle the matter that he ignored the fact that the sale did indeed violate the antitrust act.

Although the president may have favored business in this situation, he did not please all businessmen. They were eager to say, "I told you so" and to blame government regulation of industry for the depression of 1907. They fought against Roosevelt's insistence on more, not less, government regulation.

In 1906 and 1907, Roosevelt focused on some problems and projects with international significance. At the time, Japanese and Americans had already clashed over fishing rights off the coast of Alaska. Japan was building a strong military force. Some European journalists predicted that Japan might be preparing to extend its territory into the Pacific and eastward to the United States.

About seventy-five thousand Japanese lived in the United States, many of them farm laborers who offered to work for lower wages than most American workers. Some Americans resented these Japanese. In October 1906, the San Francisco school board ordered that Japanese students attend segregated schools especially established for them.

Japan was furious at this ruling, and so was Roosevelt. In his annual message to Congress in December, Roosevelt demanded that San Francisco withdraw that ruling. He took out his big stick. If California officials closed the schools to any students, he would open them, using military troops if necessary.

In February 1907, Roosevelt secretly met with a delegation from San Francisco. The mayor of San Francisco agreed to lift the prohibition against Japanese students. In return, the Japanese government agreed to stop emigration of farm laborers to California. Without these agreements, relations between the U.S. and Japan would have become much worse.

In another international project in 1907, the president announced plans to send sixteen new battleships, all painted white, and twelve thousand officers and men on a round-the-world tour. He called the tour of this "Great White Fleet" a display of American good will. It was also meant to show Japan how powerful America was.

Isolationists, including many congressmen, argued that there was no reason for America to extend itself onto the international scene. Others protested the use of the navy, a military force, as an expression of peace. The question came to a vote in Congress, which refused to appropriate money for the tour.

Roosevelt defended the tour with a quote from our first president, George Washington: "In time of peace, prepare for war." He declared that he would carry out his plan with or without congressional support. He had enough money in the budget to send the fleet to the Pacific, and he would do so. Once the ships had completed the tour, Congress could decide whether or not to bring them back. If legislators would not allocate money, then the ships would stay in the Pacific! Congress voted to bring the ships back.

In his annual message to Congress in December 1907, the president focused on domestic issues. He urged a federal income tax (in those days, people in some states paid a state income tax, but no citizen paid a federal income tax), stronger regulation of railroad rates, compulsory investigation of labor disputes in interstate commerce, and extension of the eight-hour day to more workers. These actions would help to ensure a square deal for all citizens. He repeated his belief that the poor economic climate had been created by lack of government regulation and by

President and Mrs. Roosevelt (1908).

Roosevelt's head along with those of Washington, Jefferson, and Lincoln at Mount Rushmore.

dishonest businessmen. These statements widened a conflict between Roosevelt and Republicans who opposed such reforms.

In one of his last acts as president, Roosevelt signed the Declaration of Governors along with leaders of all thirty-six states and territories. This declaration said in part: "We agree that the sources of national wealth exist for the benefit of the People." The leaders pledged to keep large areas of water and land free and available to the public, safe from private control. Roosevelt had fought long and hard for this policy. He called this "one of the most fundamentally important documents ever laid before the American people."

This declaration was one more success story in Roosevelt's conservation presidency. In all, he created five national parks, encompassing forty-three million acres of land, and sixteen national monuments, among them the Grand Canyon. Between 1903 and 1909, he created fifty-one wildlife refuges. He had also pressured Congress to grant money to irrigate three million acres in the dry West so farmers could grow crops there.

It is partly for Roosevelt's role as conservationist that the Mount Rushmore National Memorial in South Dakota features a carving of his head

A close-up of Roosevelt's head at Mount Rushmore.

(sixty feet from forehead to chin) beside the heads of Abraham Lincoln, George Washington, and Thomas Jefferson. The likeness of Roosevelt was finished in 1941.

At the Republican presidential convention in June 1908, Roosevelt refused to run again, keeping the promise he made in his 1904 victory speech. Although he admitted, "I should like to have stayed on in the Presidency," he would not change his self-imposed decision against a third term. He wrote to his son Ted, Jr.: "I have enjoyed myself in the White House more than I have ever known any other President to enjoy himself." Using the simplified spelling which he had always endorsed, he added, "I am going to enjoy myself thoroly when I leave."

Nevertheless, when he was introduced as head of the party, delegates clapped, shouted, cheered, waved teddy bears, and swung their coats around their heads for almost an hour before the chairman could gavel them to quiet. They demonstrated in vain: Roosevelt would not break his pledge.

Roosevelt had earlier decided to support William Howard Taft, his secretary of war, as his successor. He believed that Taft would be the most likely candidate to follow Roosevelt's programs and policies. Now he worked with his usual energy to get Taft elected.

The contrast between the two men was astounding. Taft was a three-hundred-pound man who was known to sleep and eat too much. He was easy-going, with none of Roosevelt's fire and enthusiasm. He admitted frankly, "I don't like politics."

Roosevelt had lots of advice for Taft about the campaign: "There must be nothing that looks like self-depreciation"; "Do not answer Bryan [Taft's opponent]; attack him!"; "Let the audience see you smile always." He advised Taft to try to keep stories of his frequent fishing and golf vacations out of the newspapers. He also wrote several long letters of endorsement for him.

On November 3, 1908, William Howard Taft was elected president, and James Sherman was elected vice-president.

Roosevelt would be an ex-president in four months. Congress no longer feared the big stick of the presidency. Roosevelt no longer had anything to gain from pleasing Congress.

Roosevelt took advantage of the situation to scold, nag, and criticize legislators. He called them selfish, accusing them of catering to their own special interests instead of working for the good of the country. He blasted them for their failure to regulate stock market investments, to provide workmen's compensation for disabled workers, and to establish penalties for dishonest businessmen.

The conflict deepened with Roosevelt's annual message to Congress in December 1908. The president criticized Congress for writing a law which reduced the power of the Secret Service. He claimed that the legislators had passed the act to protect themselves from investigation.

William Howard Taft, Roosevelt's successor as president.

Roosevelt admitted to Taft that he would be relieved to step down. On the last day of December 1908, he sent a note to the president-elect: "Ha! Ha! *You* are making up your Cabinet. *I* in a lighthearted way have spent the morning testing the rifles for my African trip."

Roosevelt was not completely lighthearted. In January, he went back to Congress with slightly modified remarks against the legislators' attitude toward the Secret Service. Angry lawmakers did not accept the modifications. They called for a vote to reject the president's comments. Two hundred eleven members voted for rejection; only thirty-six voted against it. This was the first time in eighty years that Congress had censured a president in this way.

After that censure, neither the president nor the representatives attempted to support each other.

Congress authorized a private power project in Missouri. Roosevelt vetoed the measure.

The Senate ordered an investigation of the president's emergency fund. (It found no irregularities.)

Congress created four thousand positions in the Census Bureau which would not require competitive examinations. Roosevelt vetoed the bill.

The president sent to the House of Representatives the Report of the Country Life Commission, a committee he had appointed to study farm conditions. Legislators refused to allocate funds to publish it.

As his presidency ended, Roosevelt was proud that he had brought many issues to public attention: labor rights vs. management responsibilities; the concept of the square deal; corruption in business and politics; the need for conservation of resources; government regulation of businesses; the importance of military strength. On the international scene, he had won the Nobel Peace Prize and planned the voyage of the Great White Fleet.

He had also disappointed some citizens and groups. Some Americans,

The Roosevelt family upon leaving the White House in 1909.
From left: Ethel, Kermit, Quentin, Edith, Ted, Theodore,
Archie, Alice Roosevelt Longworth, Nicholas Longworth.

particularly Westerners, felt that Roosevelt gave the federal government too much power over the states. Roosevelt had imposed federal regulations over the West's most important assets—railroads, forests, and open land. Some politicians blamed him for weakening the party system by fighting against patronage. Labor leaders praised him for encouraging unionism, but criticized him because he opposed "closed shops" (in which employees are required to be union members) and approved the use of injunctions (federal court orders) to force strikers back to work.

Many business leaders condemned him for lack of flexibility. They hoped that the new president would be more willing to listen to them.

But most Americans agreed with President Taft, who said Roosevelt would "take his place in history with Washington and Lincoln."

Chapter 14
From Republican to Progressive

What challenge was left for Roosevelt? He had already been a rancher, assemblyman, author, head of Civil Service, president of the New York City police board, assistant secretary of the navy, colonel of a fighting force, governor of New York, vice-president, and president! When he left the White House, he was fifty years old, now totally blind in one eye, considerably overweight, and still bothered by a touch of the fever he had contracted in Cuba.

He found his challenge in an African expedition to study plants and animals and to bring back specimens for the Smithsonian Institution. He would begin his trip in March, three weeks after Taft's inauguration. Edith worried that the trip would be a terrible physical strain for him. However, she admitted that strain would be "a cheap price to pay for any journey which can interest him after the life he has led for eight years."

Many publishers offered to finance the trip if he would write articles for them in return. Roosevelt accepted a $50,000 offer from *Scribner's Magazine*.

Twenty-year-old Kermit took a leave from Harvard to join him.

This cartoon shows Roosevelt on the campaign trail in June 1912, "firing away" at wrongdoing.

Roosevelt's sister Corinne prepared a traveling library for her brother. She ordered about sixty books trimmed to pocket size and bound in sturdy pigskin. The "Pigskin Library" included several books that Roosevelt asked for specifically: the Bible, some Shakespeare, some poetry and essays, and *Alice in Wonderland*. A few of the books were written in French.

As the ship *Hamburg* left the New York dock on March 23, 1909, Roosevelt stood on deck in his military uniform and waved to the crowds who had come to see him off.

The study group traveled through Kenya and over Lake Victoria to the White Nile, the home of square-mouthed rhinoceroses, crocodiles, and swarms of mosquitoes and tsetse flies.

Two hundred native porters carried the laboratory and taxidermy equipment including four tons of salt to cure skins. Roosevelt established the rule that animals would be shot only as museum specimens or for food. Safari workers followed a rigid procedure of skinning, removing and packing bones for later assembly, and cooking or disposing of meat.

Roosevelt had three excellent rifles, one of them specially fitted to accommodate his poor eyesight. He was determined to bag five of the most dangerous game—elephant, rhinoceros, buffalo, leopard, and lion. He was successful. During the trip he shot almost three hundred specimens including eight elephants, nine lions, and thirteen rhinoceroses. He kept about a dozen of these for himself. The rest were used for meat or preserved for the Smithsonian. Historians do not know if Roosevelt kept his promise to shoot no more animals than necessary.

He also sent back articles to the United States, some of which were later included in his book *African Game Trails*. In six weeks, he wrote about forty-five thousand words, fourteen articles in all.

In June 1910, Roosevelt returned to America and a glorious reunion with family and friends.

Kermit and his father with Roosevelt's first African buffalo. Its head can still be seen at Sagamore Hill.

He came back to a disturbing political situation. The popular magazine *Life* greeted him with a poem:

> Teddy, come home and blow your horn,
> The sheep's in the meadow, the cow's in the corn.
> The boy you left to 'tend the sheep
> Is under the haystack fast asleep.

Taft was not asleep, but many Republicans complained that he had not kept a promise he had made in the 1908 presidential campaign. Taft had pledged tariff reform with lower rates for imported goods. Consumers looked forward to lower prices as a result. However, as president, Taft allowed business lobbyists to push through a bill in Congress which did little to change the tariff fees.

Some Republican congressmen objected to Taft's handling of the tariff issue. They also disagreed with Taft's support of injunctions against strikers and criticized his appointment of five corporation lawyers to Cabinet positions. They believed that these decisions showed that Taft favored business over the interests of common citizens.

The new president signed bills allowing the construction of dams on land that Roosevelt had set aside as wilderness areas. Even more discouraging, Taft had fired Gifford Pinchot, Roosevelt's trusted chief forester. Taft claimed that Pinchot did not support his policies. Pinchot claimed that his replacement, Richard Ballinger, was a friend of special interest groups.

Taft admitted to Roosevelt, "I have had a hard time." Roosevelt promised not to interfere: "I shall make no speeches or say anything for two months."

He kept the promise for about ten days. Then he began to criticize, first to close friends, and then publicly.

Soon Roosevelt was active again in politics. He supported a bill to change election procedures in New York State (it failed); offered to be chairman of the Republican state convention (he was turned down); and

On Roosevelt's return, both he and the country wondered
what he could do next. Here the lion says, "I wish I knew
what you are going to do with me," and Roosevelt replies,
"So do I." "So do we," say Uncle Sam and the elephant
(the Republican party).

Roosevelt and his pilot prepare to take off in October 1910.

endorsed a candidate for governor of New York (the candidate lost).

In the summer and fall of 1910, he made a speaking tour through the West. Roosevelt supported congressional candidates described as *progressive,* meaning they believed that government leaders and citizens could work together against corruption and special interests to help the poor and weak. He introduced the concept of "New Nationalism": that public welfare must override private interests. He criticized Taft's policies. Citizens wondered if Roosevelt was beginning a campaign for his own reelection. The *New York American* asked him openly, using simplified spelling: "T.R.: R U or R U not?"

Roosevelt found adventure as he campaigned. He even flew in an airplane, something no other ex-president or president had done. He was in the air for a little over three minutes in Missouri. "It was the finest experience I have ever had," said Roosevelt. "I wish I could stay up for an hour, but I haven't time this afternoon."

He also enjoyed his automobile trips from his home to New York City, where he worked as editor of the magazine *Outlook.* He wrote of "driving the motor to and from New York with great vigor."

Supporters of progressive ideas, both Democrats and Republicans, did well in the 1910 congressional elections.

Throughout 1911, Roosevelt continued to stay in the public eye, supporting reform and denouncing Taft. He was not the only Republican to criticize Taft. In June, Senator Robert La Follette announced that he wanted to be the Republican candidate for president in 1912. La Follette headed the National Progressive Republican League, which supported many of the reforms Roosevelt endorsed.

In February 1912, Roosevelt announced that he would accept the Republican nomination for president if it was offered. He was ready to oppose Taft because he believed that the president did not listen to the American people.

Roosevelt told what he would do if he were president. He would see to it that poor children in New York City did not have to march up and down the streets begging for food and shelter. He would help United States businessmen in Mexico who complained of persecution by the Mexican government. He would try to help officials of the Standard Oil Company who struggled against strong foreign competition. He would study the situation at U.S. Steel where workers complained about low wages and poor working conditions.

Further, Roosevelt accused Taft of handling international relations with more concern for world peace than for American interests. He complained that Taft allowed business interests to buy forest lands that Roosevelt had declared noncommercial. The candidates disagreed on the most effective way to deal with mergers and trusts.

Taft used the power of the presidency to criticize Roosevelt. In October 1911, his attorney general began proceedings to overturn the 1907 merger of U.S. Steel and the Tennessee Coal and Iron Company. Taft declared that Roosevelt had violated the Sherman Antitrust Act by approving this merger.

President Taft resented Roosevelt's criticism. He said, "I hardly think the prophet of the square deal is playing it exactly square with me now." He asked Roosevelt about his pledge not to seek a third term as president. That statement applied to three terms in a row, Roosevelt answered. He compared serving three terms to drinking three cups of coffee. Stopping after two cups doesn't mean that I will never again drink another cup, he said.

Roosevelt also answered a question about party loyalty: would he support the winner of the Republican nomination, no matter who it was? He promised that he would.

Roosevelt toured the country, pounding his chest and roaring out his message of reform. Audiences stood and cheered as he shouted: "We progressives believe that human rights are supreme over all other rights . . . [and we must] free our government from the control of money in politics." He bellowed, "I'm feeling like a bull moose!" just as he had said when he was campaigning for McKinley in 1900.

As the campaign continued, Taft expressed confusion, disappointment, anger, and finally sorrow over Roosevelt's opposition. Once a reporter found Taft alone and weeping. "Roosevelt was my closest friend," he said.

By the end of May 1912, Roosevelt and Taft had about the same number of delegates to vote at the Chicago convention to choose the party's candidate for president. Then slowly but steadily, Taft pulled ahead. Some experienced politicians believed that Roosevelt had lost his political skill and popular appeal. They also said that the Republican party was solidly conservative, and that it did not share Roosevelt's belief in the need for reform.

Roosevelt believed that he was being cheated in the selection of delegates. He challenged the documents of two hundred fifty-four delegates. The Credentials Committee, controlled by Taft supporters, awarded two hundred thirty-five of those seats to Taft and only nineteen to Roosevelt.

Taft had stolen delegates! thundered Roosevelt. Historians disagree on the number of questionable delegates, but some say that a fairer committee would have accepted Roosevelt's challenges of enough delegates to create a tie between him and Taft.

Roosevelt changed his mind about supporting the Republican nominee, no matter who it was. If he lost because of inner party politics, he said, "I will have a great deal to say, and I won't stand it for a moment."

On June 17, the night before the Republican convention began, Roosevelt stood in front of five thousand fans as they shouted, stamped, and tossed their hats into the air. He told them what they wanted to hear.

"Victory will be ours," he promised. "We battle for the Lord."

On June 22, three hundred forty-four Roosevelt delegates refused to vote in what they considered a crooked election. The vote was taken anyway. Taft got 561 votes; Roosevelt, 107; La Follette, 41.

Taft was once again the Republican presidential candidate, and he had a strong following.

However, even as Taft's victory was announced, a Roosevelt rally was in full swing at a nearby hall. The three hundred forty-four delegates who had refused to vote were meeting with other Roosevelt supporters to form a new party, the Progressive party. When Roosevelt arrived, they asked him to run as their presidential candidate. He answered, "If you wish me to make the fight, I will make it." Immediately, some supporters gave the new party a nickname: the Bull Moose party.

On July 2, the Democrats nominated Woodrow Wilson, a former college professor, as their presidential candidate. Wilson disagreed with Roosevelt on monopolies. Wilson wanted monopolies to be outlawed. Roosevelt wanted them to be regulated. Wilson declared that his "New Freedom" policies would restrict monopolies by encouraging competition. He said that, in contrast, Roosevelt's New Nationalism deprived business leaders of the right and responsibility to govern themselves. Like Roosevelt, Wilson also promised protection of unions, better conditions for workers, and reforms in the banking system.

On August 5, more than ten thousand delegates at the Progressive national convention learned a new song, "I Want to Be a Bull Moose." They supported establishment of minimum health and safety standards in factories, minimum wage and maximum hour standards for women, the eight-hour day and six-day week for workers, and an end to child labor. They also favored women's suffrage, a federal income tax, and limitations on campaign contributions and expenditures.

On August 7, the Progressive party officially chose Roosevelt as its

Now that Roosevelt had broken with the Republicans, cartoonists in Republican newspapers attacked him. This cartoon, captioned "On to Chicago!" shows Roosevelt dragging along an insignificant Bull Moose party.

The Bull Moose candidate speaks from an open car.

candidate for president. The party invited Jane Addams, a famous social worker and reformer, to address the meeting. This was the first time a woman had addressed the convention of a major political party in America. To the tune of "Maryland, My Maryland," the delegates sang:

> Thou wilt not cower in the dust,
> Roosevelt, O Roosevelt!
> Thy gleaming sword shall never rust,
> Roosevelt, O Roosevelt!

The Progressive candidate traveled to thirty-four states in sixty days. He spoke from the backs of trains, from automobiles, and in the streets. In Los Angeles, stores were closed and traffic stopped as two hundred thousand people lined the streets to cheer for him. In Oregon, supporters covered his path with roses.

This cartoon shows Roosevelt arrogant enough to believe he is like Moses.

The bullet-torn speech and glasses' case protected Roosevelt from the assassin.

Roosevelt accepted campaign funds from all over the country. Businessmen gave more than one million dollars. Industry leaders like George Perkins, who had investments in companies such as U.S. Steel, would benefit more from Roosevelt's attitude toward monopolies than they would from Wilson's. A laborer sent Roosevelt five dollars, a poet sent him the ten dollars he earned from selling a poem, and a veteran in an old soldier's home sent one dollar.

On October 14, Roosevelt stepped into an open automobile on his way to make a speech in Milwaukee. Suddenly, a bullet struck him in the chest. Roosevelt slumped. People in the crowd seized the would-be assassin. Roosevelt coughed and then looked to see if blood had come from his mouth. Seeing none, he decided the bullet had not hit a lung. He rose and looked at the man who had shot him. "Mad," he said. "Don't hurt the poor creature."

He refused to allow his driver to take him to the hospital. At the Milwaukee Auditorium, he said to the crowd, "Please excuse me from making a long speech. I'll do the best I can. You see, there is a bullet in my body."

He pulled his speech from an inside pocket of his coat. Raising the bullet-torn paper over his head, he said, "It takes more than that to kill a bull moose!" He spoke for an hour and a half before he went to the hospital.

Edith took the train to Chicago to join her husband in the hospital. Immediately, she took over, insisting that he stop trying to carry on political business from the hospital bed. After six days she was no longer able to keep him down. Roosevelt began campaigning again.

The man who had attempted to assassinate Roosevelt was declared insane. He died later in a hospital for the criminally demented.

On November 5, 1912, the people voted. The tally was: Wilson, six million; Roosevelt, four million; Taft, three and a half million.

Although he did not win, Roosevelt felt that the Progressive party had done well. Maybe he was already looking ahead to the 1916 election when he told the country, "The Progressive party has come to stay. . . . The battle has just begun."

For a few months, Roosevelt continued to meet with progressives and to assure citizens: "There shall be no retreat from the position we have taken. The future is surely ours."

Chapter 15
Final Battles

By January 1913, Roosevelt was working diligently on his autobiography, which was published that October. In the spring, he collaborated with Edmund Heller, a naturalist, in a two-volume work, *Life-Histories of African Game Animals.* He also wrote criticisms of art and literature, surprising many readers with his knowledge of these subjects. One friend remembered a luncheon where the ex-president quoted some French poetry, declaring that "the rhythms of archaic French are much finer and manlier than the rhythms of modern French."

He planned to travel to Rio de Janeiro, Brazil, on a lecture trip in October. When he heard of an unmapped river, the River of Doubt, flowing north from the Amazon, the fifty-four-year-old Roosevelt decided, "We will go down that unknown river!" Relatives and close friends suggested that the trip was too dangerous. He answered, "I have already lived and enjoyed as much of life as any other nine men I know . . . and if it is necessary for me to leave my remains in South America, I am quite ready to do so."

In Brazil, Roosevelt hunted jaguar and tapir, hacked his way through

A much-thinner Roosevelt on his return from Brazil.

Roosevelt and his companions after a day's hunt in Brazil.

the jungle with a machete, waded through hip-deep swamps, and studied birds, fish, animals, plants, and trees. Late into the night he sat at a table, writing articles to send back to the United States. Swarms of mosquitoes forced him to wear netting over his head and long, thick gloves on his hands and arms.

Roosevelt injured his leg seriously while traveling down the River of Doubt (later named Rio Téodoro in his honor). The accident occurred when he tried to dislodge a dugout canoe from between two rocks. An abscess developed on the wound. The infection led to jungle fever.

When his temperature rose to 105 degrees, he begged the rest of his party to leave him there. They refused.

Fighting against treacherous rapids, soaking rain, and relentless sun, the party made its way back to civilization on April 30, 1914. Roosevelt was fifty-seven pounds lighter than when he began the trip. A much weaker man, he walked with a cane. However, he was thrilled that the group had succeeded in its mission to map the river. It had a significant collection of specimens for the American Museum of Natural History, among them jaguar, armadillo, tapir, and deer. He had written much of the manuscript for his latest book, *Through the Brazilian Wilderness*. Roosevelt told the Brazilian minister of foreign affairs, "I thank you from my heart for the chance to take part in this great work of exploration."

On the way home, the ship stopped at Barbados, an island in the West Indies. There Roosevelt bought fifty books. By the time his ship reached New York Harbor less than two weeks later, he had read all of them!

In New York, Roosevelt joked with reporters about the cane: "You see I still have the big stick."

Some Progressives begged Roosevelt to run for governor in 1914. He rejected the idea. He was no longer interested in a state office.

He did agree to support Progressive candidates in state and local elections. He delivered over one hundred speeches in fifteen states. Crowds cheered him enthusiastically everywhere, but most politicians were convinced that people were cheering Roosevelt the man, not the leader of the Progressive party.

The politicians were right. On election day in November 1914, the Progressives lost in every state except California. Roosevelt concluded, "The people have had enough of all the reformers and especially me." He added, "Probably we have erred in thinking that even in this country men were a little better and more intelligent than they actually are."

Theodore Roosevelt already had another campaign in mind. In August, World War I had broken out in Europe. Many countries were drawn in, with Great Britain, France, and Russia (the Allies) arrayed against Germany, Austria-Hungary, Turkey, and Bulgaria (the Central Powers). President Wilson announced that the United States would not become involved, and Roosevelt agreed with him publicly at first. Privately, he wrote to a friend that if he were president, he would send U.S. troops abroad right away.

Roosevelt had concealed his feelings toward the war for three months while he campaigned for Progressive candidates. After the election, he declared, "I have done everything this fall that everybody has wanted. This election makes me an absolutely free man. Thereafter I am going to say and do just what I damned please."

Immediately, he criticized Wilson for staying neutral and for failing to increase America's military strength.

He had no reservations about disagreeing with the president. Wilson had lost any potential Roosevelt support in April when he approved a treaty with Colombia expressing "sincere regret" for America's role in the Panama revolution in 1903. Further, Wilson agreed to pay the Colombians twenty-five million dollars for the territory taken from them during the term of President Theodore Roosevelt. The ex-president stormed, "Every action we took was in accordance with the highest principles of public and private morality."

Roosevelt believed that he was cleared of charges of aggression against Colombia when the Senate rejected the treaty later that year. However, in 1921, the Harding administration paid the twenty-five-million-dollar settlement.

By early 1915, Roosevelt was determined to persuade the American people to enter the war. He wrote and spoke on this topic to anyone who would read or listen.

Edith and Theodore Roosevelt (about 1915).

The German ruler warned Americans against traveling on ships owned by the Allies. He knew that Allied soldiers and supplies were being transported in ships disguised as commercial vessels. He said that the Central Powers could not be expected to search every vessel for Americans before attacking it.

Roosevelt was enraged. He believed that Americans should be able to travel safely anywhere they wanted to go.

"It makes my blood boil," he lamented. "Lord, how I would like to be president."

In May 1915, a German submarine sank the elegant British ocean liner the *Lusitania*. The ship had been sailing off the coast of Ireland, an area which the Germans considered a war zone. One hundred twenty-eight Americans were among those killed. Roosevelt demanded that President Wilson seize German ships and prohibit all trade with Germany in retaliation. Wilson did not act. He continued to hope for peace without American involvement.

Others in the United States had no such hopes. In the summer of 1915, Major-General Leonard Wood organized a military training camp for volunteers at Plattsburgh, New York. Three Roosevelt sons—Ted, Archie, and Quentin—enrolled immediately. (Kermit was in South America, working for a bank.)

Citizens debated about Wilson's failure to act. Was he afraid of war? Or did he believe that the United States could end the war by negotiating in peace?

Whatever the reason, those who favored entering the war were determined to reelect a new president in 1916. When Roosevelt was asked if he would run, he answered, "It would be a mistake to nominate me unless the country has in its mood something of the heroic."

On June 10, 1916, the Republicans nominated Supreme Court Justice Charles Evans Hughes for president. The Progressives nominated Roosevelt as the Bull Moose candidate on the same day. Roosevelt declined the nomination. If he ran and lost, Wilson would win again. Roosevelt could not accept this possibility. So he asked his supporters to work for Hughes, and he agreed to do the same. He hoped that a combined Republican/Progressive vote would beat Wilson.

Roosevelt spoke to the Progressives: "With all my heart, I shall continue to work for [these] great ideals." And he did. Observers said that Roosevelt campaigned harder than Hughes, the man whom he supported. He traveled widely in his private railroad car. Large crowds met him everywhere. In Chicago, eighteen thousand people, many waving small American flags, cheered and stamped their feet for a full half-hour before they allowed Roosevelt to speak.

The presidential election that fall was one of the closest in American history. Wilson was the winner.

Roosevelt blasted Wilson and his supporters. "The people should stand behind the President only when he is right!" he declared.

For more than a year, Roosevelt had been drawing up plans for a volunteer division to fight in Europe. As the war grew more intense, Roosevelt bombarded Secretary of War Newton Baker with requests to serve his country. He even offered to pay for the division himself until Congress declared war. He was rejected each time.

Roosevelt also wrote to the French and British ambassadors to the United States. He asked if his American division could fight under a French or British flag.

Before he received an answer, a new crisis arose. In March, German submarines sank three American ships. Fifteen lives were lost. Now Wilson had no choice. On April 2, 1917, he asked Congress for a declaration of war.

Roosevelt felt that he had no choice, either. He simply had to take part in the war. Unfortunately for him, only one man could grant him permission to take a division abroad. That person was Woodrow Wilson. Roosevelt swallowed his pride and visited the president.

Wilson spoke pleasantly with Roosevelt, but he refused permission. The president explained to the public, "Colonel Roosevelt is a splendid man and a patriotic citizen, but he is not a military leader."

Roosevelt found other ways to support the war. Speaking all over the country, he urged Americans to stand behind their fighting men. He also attended fund-raising programs. At one such benefit, the sponsors charged fifty cents to anyone who wanted to shake hands with the ex-president!

In February 1918, Roosevelt was hospitalized for abscesses. After an

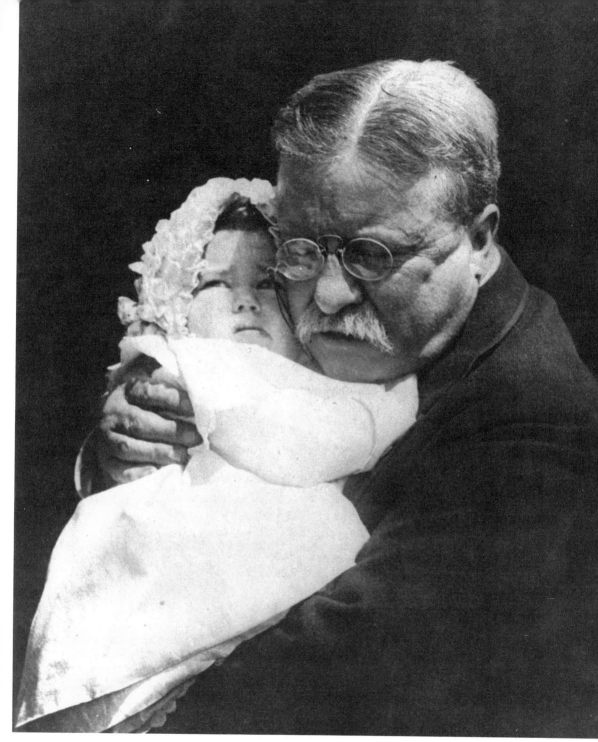

*Roosevelt and his grandchild Edith Roosevelt Derby
(Ethel's daughter). This is believed to be his last photograph.*

operation, his health failed to the point where the *New York Tribune* published an editorial: "Theodore Roosevelt—listen! You must be up and well again; we could not run this world without you."

When he returned to Sagamore Hill, he was half-deaf as well as blind in one eye. Nevertheless, he continued to make speaking tours for the war effort.

All four Roosevelt sons fought in the war. Archie and Ted were both wounded. In July, Roosevelt learned that his youngest son, Quentin, a pilot, was dead. He had been shot down behind enemy lines. A few minutes after the grieving father told Edith, he issued a statement to the press: "Quentin's mother and I are very glad that he got to the front and had a chance to render some service to his country and to show the stuff there was in him before his fate befell him."

The day after the news of Quentin's death, Roosevelt was scheduled to speak at the Republican state convention. The Republicans intended to ask him to run for election as governor. Once again, Roosevelt turned down the nomination. He did not want to be burdened with the duties of governor if he was called on to run for president in the next election. He told his sister Corinne, "I have only one fight left in me, and I think I should reserve my strength in case I am needed in 1920."

By late September 1918, it was clear that Germany was losing. Peace would soon come. But the price had been high. The United States had lost over one hundred thousand men. The casualty list for all countries totaled almost ten million men killed and twenty million wounded, in addition to countless civilians. All over the world, people wanted to make sure that such a war would never again take place.

Roosevelt attacked President Wilson's plans for a League of Nations to promote a lasting peace. He objected strongly to including former enemy nations in the League. These nations, he said, had already proven that they would violate "not only every treaty but every rule of

Theodore Roosevelt is buried at Oyster Bay in January 1919.

civilized warfare and of international good faith." He continued, "Let us dictate peace by the hammering of guns, and not talk about peace to the accompaniment of the clicking of typewriters."

On November 11, 1918, the Germans surrendered. That same day, Roosevelt entered the hospital, seriously ill with inflammatory rheumatism. Doctors told him that he might have to be in a wheelchair for the rest of his life. He answered, "All right! I can work that way, too."

He brushed off family and friends who expressed sympathy. He said, "Have you known any man who has gotten as much out of life as I have? I have seen more than any other man. I have made the very most out of my life."

Roosevelt was also content with his family life. He looked forward eagerly to visits from his five children, their husbands and wives, and his eight grandchildren. He also enjoyed quiet times with Edith. They spent many pleasant hours in the small library at Sagamore Hill, reading, writing, and talking.

Charles William Beebe, a naturalist, remembered a nighttime custom at Sagamore Hill. Roosevelt and his visitors spent some time star-watching on the lawn. As bedtime approached, they would search for the constellation Andromeda. Then they would find the faint spot of light-mist in Andromeda which indicated a galaxy. Roosevelt would recite:

> That is the spiral galaxy in Andromeda.
> It is as large as the Milky Way.
> It is one of a hundred million galaxies.
> It is 750,000 light years away.
> It consists of one hundred billion suns, each larger than our sun.

Then he would grin and say, "Now I think we are small enough. Let's go to bed."

On January 5, 1919, the sixty-year-old ex-president dictated letters, reviewed a book on birds, and wrote editorials. The next morning he died in his sleep of a blood clot in the coronary artery.

The news flashed around the world. Taft wired: "We have lost. . . the most commanding personality in our public life since Lincoln." The vice-president said, "Death had to take him sleeping, for if Roosevelt had been awake, there would have been a fight." Planes from the base where Quentin had trained dropped laurel wreaths at Sagamore Hill in honor of his father. Americans mourned, publicly and privately.

The funeral was held in the wooden chapel at Oyster Bay. About five hundred mourners crowded together for the short service. Edith, following the custom of widows, remained at Sagamore Hill where she read the funeral service.

The simple oak coffin was lowered into the earth in a burial site overlooking Oyster Bay.

Those who grieved may have found some solace remembering what Roosevelt had believed: "In the nature of things we must soon die anyhow—and we have warmed both hands before the fire of life."

Books by Theodore Roosevelt

The tireless Theodore Roosevelt wrote many books; some are mentioned in the text. Here is a list of books published by him during his lifetime. Collections of his speeches and articles assembled by others also exist.

1882	**The Naval War of 1812**
1885	**Hunting Trips of a Ranchman**
1887	**Life of Thomas Hart Benton**
1888	**Gouverneur Morris**
1888	**Ranch Life and the Hunting-Trail**
1889–96	**The Winning of the West**
1891	**New York**
1893	**The Wilderness Hunter**
1895	**Hero Tales from American History (with Henry Cabot Lodge)**
1897	**American Ideals and Other Essays Social and Political**
1899	**The Rough Riders**
1900	**Oliver Cromwell**
1900	**The Strenuous Life**
1905	**Outdoor Pastimes of an American Hunter**
1910	**African Game Trails**
1913	**Theodore Roosevelt: An Autobiography**
1913	**History as Literature and Other Essays**
1914	**Life-Histories of African Game Animals (with Edmund Heller)**
1914	**Through the Brazilian Wilderness**
1915	**America and the World War**
1916	**A Book-Lover's Holidays in the Open**
1916	**Fear God and Take Your Own Part**
1917	**The Foes of Our Own Household**
1918	**The Great Adventure**

This list provided courtesy of Wallace Finley Dailey, Curator, Theodore Roosevelt Collection, Harvard College Library.

Chronology

1858	*Theodore Roosevelt, Jr. is born.*
1860	Abraham Lincoln is elected president.
1861	The Civil War begins.
1863	Lincoln issues the Emancipation Proclamation.
1864	Lincoln is reelected president.
1865	The Civil War ends.
	Lincoln is assassinated.
	Teedie opens his Roosevelt Museum of Natural History.
1867	*Teedie writes "Natural History on Insects."*
1868	Ulysses Grant is elected president.
1869–70	*Teedie tours Europe with his family.*
1872	Grant is reelected president.
1872–73	*Teedie tours the Middle East with his family.*
1876	*Roosevelt enters Harvard.*
1877	*Roosevelt publishes a pamphlet, "The Summer Birds of the Adirondacks."*
	After a close election, Rutherford Hayes is declared president.
1880	*Roosevelt graduates from Harvard.*
	Roosevelt marries Alice Hathaway Lee.
	Roosevelt joins the Republican party.
	James Garfield is elected president.
1881	President Garfield is shot.
	Chester Arthur becomes president.
	Roosevelt is elected to the first of three terms in the New York State Assembly.
1882	The Naval War of 1812 *is published.*
1883	*Governor Cleveland asks Roosevelt to help with civil service reform.*
	The Pendleton Act is passed, providing the foundation for the present federal Civil Service.
	Roosevelt buys the Maltese Cross Ranch in North Dakota.
1884	*Alice Lee Roosevelt is born.*
	Roosevelt's mother, Mittie, and wife, Alice, die.
	Roosevelt takes a prominent part in the Republican National Convention.
	Roosevelt refuses a nomination for a fourth Assembly term.
	Grover Cleveland is elected president.
1884–1886	*Roosevelt buys the Elkhorn Ranch. He ranches in North Dakota.*
1885	Hunting Trips of a Ranchman *is published.*

1886   Deaths and injuries result from a bomb explosion in Chicago's Haymarket Square during a labor rally.

Roosevelt loses the race for mayor of New York City.

Roosevelt marries Edith Kermit Carow.

1887   Life of Thomas Hart Benton *is published.*

Theodore Roosevelt, Jr. is born.

The Boone and Crockett Club is created.

1888   Gouverneur Morris *is published.*

Ranch Life and the Hunting-Trail *is published.*

Essays in Practical Politics *is published.*

Benjamin Harrison is elected president.

1889   *Roosevelt becomes Civil Service commissioner in Washington, D.C.*

Kermit Roosevelt is born.

The Winning of the West *(vols. 1 and 2) is published.*

1890   The Sherman Antitrust Act is passed.

1891   *Ethel Roosevelt is born.*

New York *is published.*

1892   Workers at the Carnegie Steel Company in Homestead, Pennsylvania, go on strike.

Grover Cleveland is reelected president.

1893   The Wilderness Hunter *is published.*

1894   *Archibald Roosevelt is born.*

Workers at the Pullman railway sleeping car company go on strike.

1894–1896   The Winning of the West *(vols. 3 and 4) is published.*

1895   *Roosevelt becomes a police commissioner in New York City.*

1896   William McKinley is elected president.

1897   *Roosevelt becomes assistant secretary of the navy.*

Commodore George Dewey becomes commander in the Pacific.

Quentin Roosevelt is born.

American Ideals and Other Essays Social and Political *is published.*

1898   The USS *Maine* explodes in the harbor at Havana, Cuba.

The Spanish-American War begins.

Roosevelt resigns from the navy to lead the Rough Riders.

Roosevelt leads the Rough Riders in battle.

Spain surrenders; the Spanish-American War ends.

Roosevelt is elected governor of New York.

1899	The Rough Riders *is published.*
1900	McKinley is reelected president.
	Roosevelt is elected vice-president.
1901	McKinley is assassinated.
	Roosevelt becomes president.
1902	*Roosevelt invokes the Sherman Antitrust Act against the Northern Securities Company.*
	Roosevelt mediates the Pennsylvania coal strike.
	Roosevelt receives congressional permission to negotiate with Colombia for land for a canal.
	The "teddy bear" is invented.
	Roosevelt mediates Venezuela's dispute with Germany and Great Britain.
1903	The Elkins Act, regulating railroads in interstate commerce, is passed.
	Panamanian rebels win independence from Colombia with U.S. help.
1904	The Russo-Japanese War begins.
	Roosevelt is reelected president.
	Roosevelt states his corollary to the Monroe Doctrine.
1905	Work begins on the Panama Canal.
	Roosevelt injures his left eye during boxing practice.
	Roosevelt creates the U.S. Forest Service.
	Roosevelt mediates a settlement between Russia and Japan.
1906	*Alice Roosevelt marries Congressman Nicholas Longworth.*
	Upton Sinclair's The Jungle is published.
	The Hepburn Act further regulates railroads.
	The Pure Food and Drug Act and the Meat Inspection Act are passed.
	Racial conflict erupts in Brownsville, Texas.
	San Francisco orders separate schools for Japanese students.
	Roosevelt is awarded the Nobel Peace Prize.
1907	*Roosevelt mediates conflict between San Franciscans and the Japanese.*
	Roosevelt creates twenty-one forest reserves.
	A stock market drop creates economic panic.
	United States Steel buys the Tennessee Coal and Iron Company.
	The Great White Fleet begins its world tour.
1908	The Declaration of Governors promises to protect national resources from private control.
	William Howard Taft is elected president.
1909	*Roosevelt is censured by Congress.*
	Roosevelt travels to Africa to hunt.
1910	*Roosevelt introduces the "New Nationalism."*
	African Game Trails *is published.*

1912	The Republican party chooses Taft over Roosevelt as its presidential candidate.
	The Progressive party nominates Roosevelt as its presidential candidate.
	A would-be assassin shoots Roosevelt.
1913	Theodore Roosevelt: An Autobiography *is published.*
1913–1914	*Roosevelt hunts in Brazil.*
1914	*Roosevelt rejects the Progressives' request to run for New York State governor.*
	World War I begins.
	The Panama Canal is opened to traffic.
	Life-Histories of African Game Animals *is published.*
	Through the Brazilian Wilderness *is published.*
1915	German submarines sink the British liner *Lusitania*.
1916	*Roosevelt rejects the Progressive presidential nomination.*
	Wilson is reelected president.
1917	The U.S. declares war on the Central Powers.
	Wilson refuses to let Roosevelt command a division.
1918	*Roosevelt is hospitalized for treatment of abscesses.*
	Quentin Roosevelt is killed in the war.
	World War I ends.
1919	*Theodore Roosevelt dies.*

Photo Credits

Bibliography

Many books have been written about Theodore Roosevelt. In addition, both Harvard College Library and the Library of Congress contain large collections of his letters, papers, and speeches. Here are some publications that were particularly useful.

Busch, Noel. *T. R. The Story of Theodore Roosevelt.* New York: Reynal, 1963.

Cahn, William. *A Pictorial History of American Labor.* New York: Crown, 1972.

Chessman, G. Wallace. *Governor Theodore Roosevelt.* Cambridge, Mass.: Harvard University Press, 1965.

Cutright, Paul. *Theodore Roosevelt, the Making of a Conservationist.* Chicago and Urbana: University of Illinois Press, 1985.

Findley, Rowe. "Our National Forests: Problems in Paradise." *National Geographic* 162 (September 1982): 307–27.

Forma, Warren. *They Were Ragtime.* New York: Grosset & Dunlap, 1976.

Gardner, Joseph. *Departing Glory.* New York: Charles Scribner's Sons, 1973.

Harbaugh, William. *The Life and Times of Theodore Roosevelt.* New York: Oxford University Press, 1975.

Hart, Albert, and Herbert Ferleger, eds. *Theodore Roosevelt Cyclopedia.* New York: Roosevelt Memorial Association, 1941.

Lorant, Stefan. *The Life and Times of Theodore Roosevelt.* New York: Doubleday, 1959.

McCullough, David. *Mornings on Horseback.* New York: Simon and Schuster, 1981.

Morris, Edmund. *The Rise of Theodore Roosevelt.* New York: Ballantine Books, 1979.

Morris, Sylvia. *Edith Kermit Roosevelt.* New York: Coward, McCann, & Geoghegan, 1980.

Pringle, Henry. *Theodore Roosevelt.* New York: Harcourt, Brace & World, 1956.

Putnam, Carleton. *Theodore Roosevelt* (vol. 1). New York: Charles Scribner's Sons, 1958.

Roosevelt, Theodore. *African Game Trails.* New York: Charles Scribner's Sons, 1922.

———. *Outdoor Pastimes of an American Hunter.* New York: Arno, 1970.

———. *Theodore Roosevelt: An Autobiography.* New York: Macmillan, 1913.

———. *The Letters of Theodore Roosevelt,* 8 vols., ed. Elting Morison et al. Cambridge, Mass.: Harvard University Press, 1951–54.

Sinclair, Upton. *The Jungle.* New York: Penguin, 1982.

Wilson, Gregory. "How Teddy Bear Got His Name." *The Washington Post Potomac* (November 30, 1969): 33–37.

Index

Boldface page numbers indicate illustrations